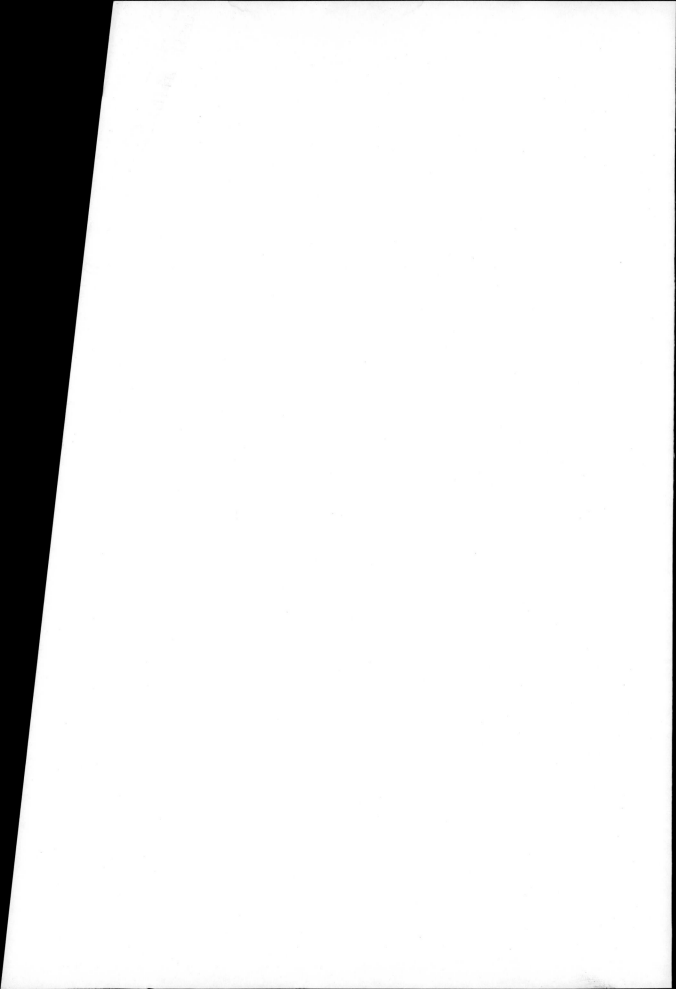

ANAKIN
SKYWALKER
THE STORY OF DARTH VADER

CHRONICLE BOOKS

SAN FRANCISCO

ANAKIN SKYWALKER

THE STORY OF DARTH VADER

By Stephen J. Sansweet

with Daniel Wallace and Josh Ling

Printed in China

Library of Congress Cataloging-in-Publication Data available.
ISBN 0-8118-2219-2

Coordinated by Lucy Autrey Wilson (Lucasfilm)
Edited by Allan Kausch (Lucasfilm) and Sarah Malarkey (Chronicle Books)

Book design by Tolleson Design
Design direction by Michael Carabetta and Julia Flagg

Distributed in Canada by Raincoast Books
8680 Cambie Street
Vancouver, BC V6P 6M9

10 9 8 7 6 5 4 3 2 1

Chronicle Books
85 Second Street
San Francisco, CA 94105

www.chroniclebooks.com

Acknowledgments

This book came together incredibly quickly once the final go-ahead was given. Darth Vader is such a great character that the manuscript, while it didn't write itself, was great fun to put together. It couldn't have been done without the hard—and concentrated—efforts of my co-authors and friends, Dan Wallace, who spun the Vader saga, and Josh Ling, the master list maker.

At Lucasfilm, thanks go to Lucy Autrey Wilson, for helping pull together all the disparate pieces of the puzzle; Allan Kausch, for his skillful editing; Cara Evangelista, who helped dig out all the art; and Tim Wills, who managed the figure side of the equation. At Hasbro, a tip of the hat to Vinnie D'Alleva, head of New Ventures, for the brainstorming session that led to the Anakin/Vader idea; and at Chronicle Books, Sarah Malarkey, who is quickly becoming a Star Wars expert; and Julia Flagg and Michael Carabetta for their design expertise, working hand in hand with Tolleson Design. The Vader collectibles were ably photographed by Steve Essig.

For those of you bold enough—or dark-side enough—to admit that Lord Vader is your favorite character in the trilogy, you're in good company. He's George Lucas's favorite too.

TABLE OF CONTENTS

I: THE EMERGENCE OF DARTH VADER

From the moment that he first appeared on screen as a nightmarish demon in black striding down a spaceship corridor, Darth Vader became an icon of evil. With his nearly seven-foot frame covered from head to toe in armor and leather, a billowing black cape that left a fleeting trace of where he had just been, and a hard-edged helmet and mask that furthered the terror, Vader didn't have to utter a word to strike fear. When he did speak, those deep, modulated tones were interrupted by harsh, mechanical breathing that further chilled his enemies. From the start, it was apparent that Darth Vader was indeed a villain for the ages.

That, of course, pleased writer-director George Lucas. What Lucas hadn't expected was how popular Darth Vader would become. The poster boy for villainy—both figuratively and literally—his was the costume that kids wanted to wear at Halloween. It was Vader's image on T-shirts, pajamas, underwear, and the like that sold the best. Editorial cartoonists quickly adopted Vader as shorthand for whatever immorality they were trying to portray. When Ronald Reagan declared that the Soviet Union was the "Evil Empire," it was Vader—not some aging, faceless Communist bureaucrat—that sprang to mind.

And yet, the character who was so easy to hate in *Star Wars*, the epitome of pure evil, became much more complex as the trilogy continued. When audiences found out the terrible, dark secret at the end of *The Empire Strikes Back*, that Vader was really Anakin Skywalker, the father of farmboy-turned-hero Luke Skywalker, millions gasped in disbelief. In fact, Lucas made sure that the dialog was written and played in such a way that younger children could believe that the dreadful line, **"I am your father,"** was really a lie if the immensity of the revelation was just too much to bear.

Opposite: The look of Darth Vader was a collaborative effort among George Lucas, Ralph McQuarrie (who did this sketch), and costume designer John Mollo.

Left: The imposing Dark Lord of the Sith makes a memorable first appearance in a smoke-filled corridor of the captured Rebel Blockade Runner in this scene from Star Wars.

0000111100101010011101101111111001010101010101000110001110100111010000011110010100011011

By the time *Return of the Jedi* rolled around, filmgoers knew that Vader had spoken the truth. Still, there was a lot more to learn about his character, something that Luke had felt long before anyone else. "Your thoughts betray you, Father," the younger Skywalker says during a break in their violent lightsaber battle in the Emperor's throne room aboard the second Death Star. "I feel the good in you . . . the conflict."

"There is no conflict," Vader insists. In the end, Luke is proven right.

Lucas says that the new *Star Wars* trilogy that he is working on now, combined with the existing three films, will in totality be the story of Anakin Skywalker and the entire Skywalker family. The "larger story of Darth Vader is a story in a more classical sense," he told Jane Paley, who interviewed him for a film and audio tour that accompanied the yearlong *Star Wars: The Magic of Myth* exhibition at the Smithsonian Institution's National Air and Space Museum. "It's about the struggle between good and evil, and about how somebody falls from grace and then is redeemed by his son."

In the first trilogy, Lucas says, we'll get to know Anakin first as a gifted nine-year-old, then as a young Jedi Knight who falls in love and marries. And we'll be witnesses to Anakin's eventual turn to the dark side of the Force, becoming the monstrous Darth Vader. It will be a mighty and wrenching fall.

In the end, with help from his son Luke, Anakin struggles and finds the last bit of the light side within himself, ultimately achieving redemption. In his first draft for *Jedi*, Lucas in fact had the elder Skywalker achieve even more—a return to his corporeal body and a reunion with Luke. In fact, all three departed Jedi—Anakin, Ben Kenobi, and Yoda—returned in the flesh. A later draft had Ben and Yoda return as shimmering images with Luke lost in deep thought about his departed father. In the shooting script by Lawrence Kasdan and Lucas and in the film, the three departed Jedi appear smiling, side by side, in their spirit forms.

Above and Right: Concept artist Ralph McQuarrie dashed off scores of quick sketches before final appearance details were settled. These sketches are of particular interest because they show a Vader with a mask but no helmet.

As many buffs know, there were lots of changes between the initial story treatments and the various drafts for all three films in the trilogy, but none more so than for *The Star Wars*, which lost its initial article after the fourth and final draft had been written. Still there are bits and pieces that foreshadow the character of Darth Vader, the Dark Lord of the Sith, from the earliest writings.

In the story treatment, completed in the spring of 1973, sixteen-year-old Annikin [sic] Starkiller is living on the fourth moon of Utapau with his ten-year-old brother Deak and his father Kane, one of the last of the Jedi. They are hiding out from the rival Knights of Sith when Annikin spots a spacecraft orbiting the moon and rushes back to his hut with the news. The three then go to investigate the strange craft, which has landed, when seemingly out of nowhere a Sith warrior appears behind the two boys and kills Deak with his long "lazersword." The warrior is dressed in black robes and wearing a face mask.

Annikin pulls out his own lazersword and engages the warrior. Kane, who had gone on in advance of his sons, rushes back and slays the Sith warrior. Kane and Annikin later use the Sith ship to escape to Aquilae and go to the underground fortress of a General Skywalker. Kane is dying and asks Skywalker to complete Annikin's training. In another echo of what would become a major facet of Darth Vader, only Kane's head and right arm are human; all the rest of his body has been supplanted by mechanical and electronic devices.

"Having machines, like the droids, that are reasonably compassionate and a man like Vader who becomes a machine and loses his compassion was a theme that interested me," Lucas told author Laurent Bouzereau in an interview for *Star Wars: The Annotated Screenplays*. The character of Annikin embodies some of the traits Lucas would later assign both to Luke Skywalker and the irascible pirate Han Solo.

THE EMERGENCE OF DARTH VADER

Darth Vader, at least in name, exists in the rough draft. So how did Lucas come up with the name itself? In an in-house interview with Lucasfilm marketing executive Charlie Lippincott four months after *Star Wars* was released, Lucas had a simple explanation.

"Darth Vader is just another one of those things that came out of thin air," Lucas said. "It sort of appeared in my head one day. I mean I had lots of Darth this and Darth that, and Dark Lord of the Sith and all those kinds of things. And then I also added lots of last names—Vaders and Wilsons and Smiths—and I just came up with combining Darth and Vader." It should be noted that Lucas had long toyed with the possibility of making Vader Luke's father, but he wasn't sure at that point whether he wanted to reveal that in the second or the third film. It seems little coincidence that, in several European languages, Darth Vader comes close to meaning "dark father."

In the *Star Wars* rough draft, General Vader isn't a very important character, just tall and scowling when he's first encountered on Alderaan, at that point the Empire's headquarters planet. He's introduced just as the ruler of the Galactic Empire announces that he is sending his troops to conquer the Aquilae system, the last remaining hideout of the Jedi.

By the screenplay's second draft, Darth Vader has emerged nearly full-blown as the character that we love to hate. But now it's Deak Starkiller who engages him. And Lucas has assigned names to the opposite sides of the Force of Others: Bogan for the dark side and Ashla for the light side. As in the film itself, Vader makes a powerful entry aboard an overtaken Rebel space fighter. It is this scene that concept artist Ralph McQuarrie used to make one of the five paintings that convinced 20th Century-Fox to give the go-ahead to the filming of *Star Wars:*

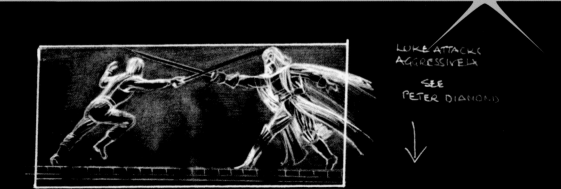

VADER
IGNITES

For an eerie moment, all is deathly quiet as a huge darker figure appears in the sub-hallway. The remaining stormtroopers bow low toward the doorway. An awesome, seven-foot BLACK KNIGHT OF THE SITH makes his way into the blinding light of the cockpit area. This is LORD DARTH VADER, right hand to the MASTER OF THE SITH. His sinister face is partially obscured by his flowing black robes and grotesque breath mask, which are in sharp contrast to the fascist white armored suits of the Imperial stormtroopers. The troops instinctively back away from the imposing warrior..

Deak Starkiller stands firm; a new look of resolve sweeps across his tired face. The smoky room is deathly quiet, except for the occasional snapping and popping of burning electrical circuits in the cockpit's sophisticated control panel.

As the Black Knight enters the corridor, the few surviving troopers scramble into the sub-hallway. Lord Vader speaks in an oddly filtered voice through his complex breathing mask.

> VADER   At last we meet!

> DEAK   With so much commotion, I expected your master, not merely a servant.

Vader is angered by this remark. Taking a deep breath, he raises his arms and every object that isn't bolted down is picked up by an invisible force and hurled at the young Jedi. When the objects reach [within] about two feet of Deak, they are deflected by an invisible shield which surrounds him.

> DEAK (CONT'D)   The Bogan is strong with you; but not nearly strong enough. I'm afraid you have to use your weapon, if you're able!

> VADER   I am Lord Darth Vader, first Knight of the Sith, and right hand to His Eminence

Prince Espaa Valorum, the Master of the Bogan. You will not mock me, or my Master; for the Ashla is weak, and the Force of Others can not save you now . . .

The fearsome dark knight ignites his lazersword and takes a defensive stance. The two galactic warriors stand perfectly still for a few moments, sizing each other up and waiting for the right moment. Deak seems to be under increasing pressure and strain, as if an invisible weight were being placed upon him. He shakes his head and blinking, tries to clear his eyes.

VADER (CONT'D)   Your powers are weak . . .

Deak makes a sudden lunge at the huge warrior but is checked by a lightning movement of the SITH. A second masterful slash-stroke by Deak is again blocked by his evil opponent.

They stand motionless for a few moments, with lazerswords locked in midair, creating a low buzzing sound. Another of the Jedi's blows is blocked, then countered. Deak stumbles back against a wall. Slowly Deak is forced to his knees as all his energy is drained from his being. Finally, he collapses in a heap. The sinister knight lets out a horrible, shrieking laugh, as stormtroopers rush in with restraining poles, followed by a braided and flashy Imperial commander. Deak's arms and legs are pinned to the wall.

The physical appearance of Darth Vader was a joint effort of Lucas, who had a mental picture of his Dark Lord of the Sith; the talented conceptual artist Ralph McQuarrie; and costume designer John Mollo, who had to translate McQuarrie's designs into workable and wearable costumes. It's fascinating to note that the look of Vader was so well conceived, so specific to the character yet so universal, that each of the three creators saw in it different influences.

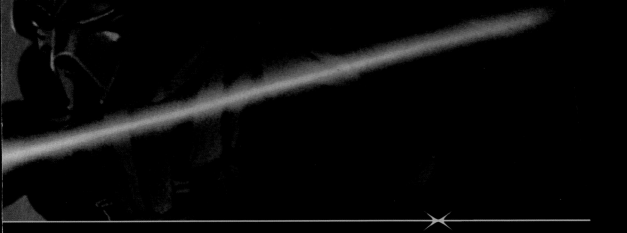

"The original idea for Darth Vader was that he was this very big, ominous, slightly technological character, but obviously very human," Lucas told interviewer Jane Paley. "I wanted a helmet that was very threatening . . . and I was inspired by Japanese helmets during the medieval period, which had a large flare on them over the shoulders." Vader's helmet was inspired by the feudal Japanese *kabuto,* its basinlike crown widening and flaring at the ears. His face mask is somewhat reminiscent of the iron, steel, or lacquered leather *mempo* of a Japanese samurai of the period. While it was primarily meant to protect a warrior's face, the *mempo* was often designed to look like some horrific beast to frighten enemies. Not surprisingly, Vader's appearance had a similar effect.

McQuarrie notes, "He was spoken of in the script as a sort of dark lord of the evil side. I thought of a guy who perhaps was sort of like a Bedouin—the Bedouin idea was rather fascinating to George with these Tusken Raiders that he had in the script and the desert setting for Tatooine. At that time, I think he had Darth Vader linked with that."

Time was of the essence in getting the first five paintings done. "In the process of inventing these things my main source of inspiration was, of course, George Lucas," McQuarrie says. "I'd read the draft and George would come and describe in a few words—a very few words—what he wanted." McQuarrie sometimes did quick pencil sketches even as Lucas spoke. "I kept reading, and listening to George, and just doing illustrations," the artist adds. "I just kept moving on, sometimes without a specific OK from George, but with me thinking a particular design looked good. And I seemed to be doing what George wanted.

"I remember George saying that Vader should have a kind of silk robe that always fluttered as he came and went, and he might have his face covered with sort of a black silk scarf and have some kind of big helmet like a Japanese warrior." McQuarrie pointed out that the first time Vader is seen, he has just emerged

Above: In one of the earliest McQuarrie pre-production paintings based on the second draft of the screenplay for The Star Wars, *a young Deak Starkiller confronts the fearsome Darth Vader.*

Left and Right: Quick sketches of a more sinister looking Vader, some of them drawn on the back of scrap letterhead paper and no more than an inch or two high, were tossed off by McQuarrie, wielding a very fluid pencil.

McQuarrie's concept design for Vader's mask and helmet had a Japanese feudal influence and was a bit more sinister than the final appearance, which included some modifications by John Mollo.

from his own spacecraft into the Rebel spaceship. "They burn through the door or something and in comes Vader when the door blows out . . . striding right in from outer space."

McQuarrie, who had worked as an illustrator for Boeing and done some Apollo animations for CBS News, said his background made him ask Lucas a question. "I said, well, gee, George, I mean how's he going to breathe out there?" McQuarrie recounts. "And George said, well, maybe for this scene we could give him some sort of breathing mask, and that everybody in the ship can have a sort of breath mask that they've slapped on. At that time Luke [actually Deak Starkiller] was going to meet Vader right there in the hallway. So I gave Luke and Vader these masks in my illustration," which was one of the original ones shown to Fox.

"George liked the mask that I did for Vader, with the big goggles and everything so he said, 'That's great, that's fine,' and we just left it at that," McQuarrie says. "That's it. You see, we weren't trying to work out every angle on this thing; we were just trying to get the general spirit of the film and go on to the next illustration quickly. All the stuff that I did on *Star Wars* I did in a relatively short time frame." Much to McQuarrie's later surprise—and delight—much of his quick conceptual work was translated almost verbatim onto the screen.

There were some changes. "The Darth that emerged in the film contrasted with my drawings in the sense that he was a more upright figure. Very stern," McQuarrie notes. "My guy was a little bit round shouldered and had more of a curving down look to his face. His mask was kind of evil looking, I think perhaps a little more sinister than the one in the film. But the film look was the correct one—that immense upright look goes along with the voice of authority. Vader isn't an evil little snakelike guy. He's a gigantic, commanding figure. He's a general."

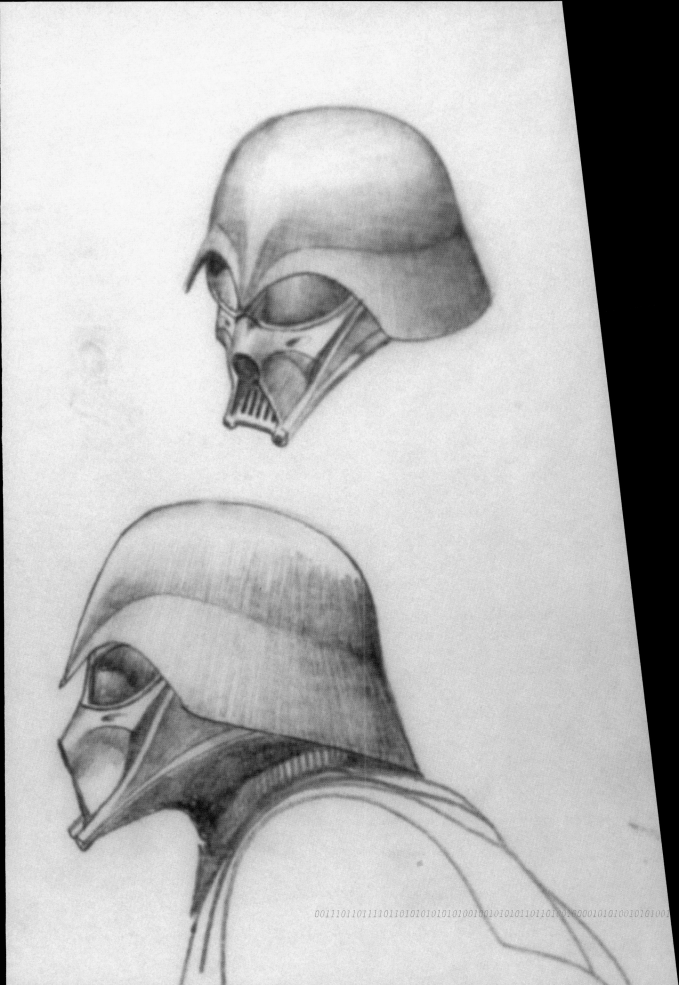

0011101101111011010101010101001001010101011011011010100001010100101010

For years, a fully dressed Darth Vader mannequin has quietly stood guard at the Lucasfilm Archives, ensuring that there are no disturbances from this galaxy or any other.

John Mollo, who won an Academy Award for his costume design for *Star Wars,* had the task of developing costumes for scores of actors and extras and also of turning the designs of Ralph McQuarrie into wearable reality. "Essentially, Ralph's sketches, which other creative departments would also rely on, took the place of historical reference for us," Mollo says.

"In the sketches, the main characters were depicted in quite small scale," he adds. "So our first step was to go to Berman's and Nathan's, the theatrical costumiers, and dress models from their stock, approximating as far as possible the appearance of the figures shown in the sketches. Then we photographed the models and showed them to George. After that, it was a matter of change and adjustment until we achieved the look they wanted."

For the first film, Mollo had only slightly more than three months to do all the costumes. "Doing it the way we did was sort of a shortcut," Mollo recalls. "We dressed our models up in whatever we could find. For instance, Darth Vader had this black sort of motorcycle suit on, a Nazi helmet, a gas mask, and a monk's cloak that we found in the Middle Ages department. And when George came to London we repeated that to put on a live fashion show and George would say, 'I like this' and 'I don't like that.' There was very little drawing done; it was really more of a practical make-do." Once the look was agreed on, Mollo and his staff constructed the actual costumes.

On Vader, in particular, some reworking was needed. "The problem was to redesign it because it was going to be made up in leather and it was going to be a very hot and very uncomfortable costume," Mollo recalls. "It was a matter of making it in certain pieces so that you could take bits off quickly on the set so that he wouldn't have to go around all day in the whole caboodle. The costumiers made the basic suit and we in the studio made the mask, the armor, the belts, and the funny boxlike thing with lights on it [on his chest]. I think Vader turned out very much like he looks in the McQuarrie sketches."

The two-part Vader mask, revealed only at the end of Return of the Jedi, *shows part of the Dark Lord's life-support system. Nearby is his Jedi weapon, a lightsaber.*

"George didn't want any fastenings to show, so we used things like Velcro and wrapped things over and tied them off with belts. For the functional-looking belts and boxes, I started going around an area in London where all the electronics firms are and buying up £20 worth of things. The shopkeepers would say, 'That doesn't go with that,' and I would tell them, 'I don't mind, you know; I'm just going to be sticking this on a robot.'"

While for McQuarrie the influence for Vader was somewhat Middle Eastern, and for Lucas Japanese, Mollo—who had developed a reputation as a military costume expert—saw it as a bit closer to home. "It was more of a Nazi influence, really," he says. "I mean to me it looks sort of like a Nazi helmet and pieces of trench armor that the Germans wore in World War I."

The appearance of the unmasked Vader at the end of *Jedi* was an important moment for the entire first trilogy. It was a physical transformation that served to punctuate his spiritual transformation. In the beginning, Lucas really wasn't focused on what that look might be, as he told Bouzereau in *Star Wars: The Annotated Screenplays*:

"I didn't have a very specific idea about what Vader might look like underneath the mask. I knew that he had been in a lot of battles, and at one point I thought that he had had a confrontation with Ben and Ben had sent him into a volcano. But he was all but dead, and basically he was manufactured back together even though there was very little left of him. So he is kind of this three-quarters mechanical man and one-quarter human, and the suit he wears is like a walking iron lung. By the time we got to the third film, we were able to articulate what Vader looked like underneath the mask, but until then I just knew that he was pretty messed up simply because he could barely breathe or speak." Still, Lucas made the important decision to make the unmasked Vader sad looking, and thus somewhat sympathetic, rather than repulsive looking as a legion of fans had come to expect.

Another important contributor to the persona of Darth Vader was Ben Burtt, Academy Award-winning sound designer, who came up with the unforgettable breathing sound that has been imitated by millions since *Star Wars* hit theaters. To get the effect of tortured breathing from Vader's ruined lungs, Burtt first tried to synthesize a unique sound composed of around eighteen types of human breathing, but that didn't work. "We learned that what we really wanted was just an icy, cold, mechanical breathing," he says. "And Darth breathing was a recording that I made. It was me breathing through the regulator on my scuba tank. Then I'd edit those breaths into every scene with Darth Vader and try to match the breathing rhythm of the speech, which of course was the voice of James Earl Jones."

Lucasfilm wanted foreign audiences to get as much benefit as possible from all the sound engineering done for *Star Wars*, so Burtt was sent to several countries to help in the dubbing process. "We had a French Darth Vader, an Italian Darth Vader, and so on," he explains. "In each case, we tried to come up with a means of processing the local actor's voice so that you got a sense of a booming voice inside a space helmet. It's important for Vader's voice to really seem as though it's coming from his helmet. He has no mouth to locate a voice, and if you just put a voice on the screen somewhere and it's supposed to be Darth Vader, there's always the problem that you don't connect the voice with that character."

Burtt says that the French mix turned out to be his favorite, both because of the equipment and the creativity of the French sound mixers. "We tried to come up with a way of processing Darth Vader's voice to get a booming effect, and we played around with a lot of different methods," he recalls. "The one we finally used was that we played Vader's voice over a speaker and then put a long stovepipe tube in front of the speaker with a microphone at the other end. The sound reverberated though the stovepipe and then was picked up by the microphone, fed out through the mixing console, and blended in the final

ANAKIN SKYWALKER: THE STORY OF DARTH VADER

soundtrack of the picture. We got a slightly metallic, booming sound to Darth's voice, which worked very well."

Burtt had a slightly different experience in Italy. "They loved Darth Vader's breathing in Italy and turned it up really loud. Every time Darth was on the screen there was this huge breathing. It sounded like a steamboat!"

While there is only one Darth Vader, it actually took four men to carry out all aspects of the role. For most of the trilogy, the man behind the mask was David Prowse, a six-foot-seven giant of a man who had won the Mr. Universe title in 1962. Prowse's most notable role until then had been that of a bodyguard for a revenge-seeking author in *A Clockwork Orange*. George Lucas offered him a choice of roles, that of Chewbacca or Darth Vader. Knowing that villains are often the most memorable characters in a film, Prowse picked Vader, not realizing until he went for costume fittings that the Dark Lord of the Sith *always* wore a helmet and face mask. (Chewbacca, of course, wouldn't have been any more revelatory.) It is Prowse who is responsible for that famous stride, the imposing presence, and the hand gestures as he inflicts unseen pain or even death on those for whom he has no more use. Prowse says his two favorite scenes are his entrance in *Star Wars* ("It's the greatest entrance that anybody can ever wish for") and the lightsaber duel with Luke Skywalker at the end of *The Empire Strikes Back*. Prowse was given dummy lines for that scene and it wasn't until he saw the completed film that he knew that Vader was Luke's father.

It was also in that scene that the second Vader was used. While Prowse had done all the fighting in *Star Wars*, the battle in *Empire* was trickier, so the production brought in stuntman Bob Anderson to do some of the swordplay on the gantry in Cloud City. Anderson reprised his role by doing all of the fighting in *Return of the Jedi*.

100101100100011000111010011101000001111001010001110110111101101010

The third and most famous Vader is the talented actor James Earl Jones, whose stentorian delivery, along with Ben Burtt's sound effects and Dave Prowse's body movements, absolutely nailed the character. Not many people know that the multi-award-winning Jones, whose voice announces "This is CNN" around the world, had to overcome a severe stuttering problem as a child. In his autobiography, *Voices and Silences,* Jones says that for a long time he used to deny that he was Vader's voice, because it was fun to do so. But the role, which took him less than three hours to do for the first film, "set off a chain reaction of voices in my career. With Darth Vader, that mythical character, my voice came to be used more and more frequently as a voice of authority." Jones also appreciates the exposure the role gave him to another generation of audiences who might not be familiar with his body of theatrical and other work.

Jones, who gives full credit to Prowse for creating the Vader persona, gave some fascinating insight into what is one of the most famous voice-overs in modern film in an interview with Pete Hull for the *Star Wars Insider.*

"For *The Empire Strikes Back* and *Return of the Jedi* we set aside the whole day, eight hours, for the looping of Vader's voice," Jones told Hull. "In *Empire,* I didn't know quite what I had done right in the first one. As an actor I wanted to improve my performance. I wanted to do a good job, to be more expressive. But we discovered that being more expressive wasn't the right approach for Vader.

"George Lucas and the others and I sat around and asked the question, 'If you deal with the voice as a musical instrument in terms of human inflection, what is Darth Vader's voice?' I think one of them then said, 'That's probably the mistake we're making. Vader doesn't express himself with his voice. The word

is there, he lays it out, and that's it. Vader is a man who never learned the beauties and subtleties of human expression.' So we figured out the key to my work was to keep it on a very narrow band. A narrow band of expression . . . that was the secret."

The fourth and final Vader from the first trilogy was Royal Shakespeare Company veteran Sebastian Shaw, then eighty-two years old. The late actor's scenes were shot at Elstree Studios on closed sets, which were cleared of all but essential crew. Shaw played Vader in the famous scene at the end of *Jedi* when audiences finally see the scarred wreck of a man who had been trapped so long behind the ebony mask. And, at the end of the film, he stands proudly and scarless next to Yoda and Alec Guinness' Obi-Wan Kenobi, all of them shimmering spirits at one with the Force.

British actor Ian McDiarmid, who played the role of Emperor Palpatine under heavy makeup, remembers the day of the shoot. "I was in for my four-hour makeup and I saw Sebastian Shaw in the corridor," he told Scott Chernoff in an interview for the *Star Wars Insider*. "I knew Sebastian quite well. I said, 'Sebastian! Good heavens! What are you doing here?' He said, 'I don't know, dear boy, I think it's something to do with science fiction.' That was Sebastian. The *Star Wars* saga had passed him blissfully by."

But all the behind-the-scenes explanations of the look, the sound, and the very *feel* of the character of Darth Vader aren't enough to explain his impact. A lot of that has to do with movie magic, the melding of the skills of a bevy of creative people so that the sum far exceeds its parts. The singular vision of George Lucas, carried out in his roles as conceptualizer, writer, and director, is another important aspect. But beyond that, what is it about Vader that has made the character such an indelible part of the last two decades of the twentieth century?

Above Left: Vader is unrelenting in his pursuit of the still not fully trained Luke Skywalker, and uses both his lightsaber and other dark-side Force powers to subdue the young Jedi.

Left: Luke Skywalker is about to make a momentous decision in his confrontation with Darth Vader in the reactor core of Bespin's Cloud City.

The answer to that may be bound up in the magic of myth, not coincidentally the title of the Smithsonian exhibit in Washington, D.C. Lucas has long said that he set out trying to create a new myth for a generation of children who had none of their own that were relevant. In the exhibition's fascinating companion book, *Star Wars: The Magic of Myth*, by Mary Henderson, the exhibit's curator asks Lucas to describe the role of myth in the creation of the *Star Wars* films:

"I was trying to take certain mythological principles and apply them to a story. Ultimately, I had to abandon that and just simply write the story. I found that when I went back and read it, then started applying it against the sort of principles that I was trying to work with originally, they were all there. . . . I'd sort of immersed myself in the principles that I was trying to pour into the script . . . [and] these things were just indelibly infused into the script."

One of those indelible myths that is part of the context of Darth Vader is the constant and momentous struggle between good and evil; another is the passing of the power of what Lucas calls the light side and the dark side from fathers to sons. Luke sets out on the hero's journey, one that will transform him, but Vader is on a journey too. He has been transformed once—from the youthful and good Anakin Skywalker into the relentlessly evil Darth Vader—but Lucas will transform him back again at the end of the journey.

Another way that Lucas tweaks mythological conventions is in the familiar plot of the hero slaying the monster. In this case, a monster, in the form of Vader, slays a hero, Obi-Wan Kenobi. But Kenobi isn't dead in the traditional sense. He has let Vader strike him down only to become one with the Force, which will allow him to continue as a guide on Luke Skywalker's difficult journey.

Above Right: Darth Vader walks down the lower deck of an Imperial landing platform on the forest moon of Endor to have another encounter with his son, Luke, who has surrendered to the crew of an Imperial walker.

Right: Darth Vader is escorted by some Imperial dignitaries as he lands his shuttle on a deck of the uncompleted second Death Star with his son, Luke, in tow. Both production paintings are by Ralph McQuarrie.

ANAKIN SKYWALKER: THE STORY OF DARTH VADER

In *The Empire Strikes Back,* Vader plays another role, as Henderson points out. When Jedi Master Yoda tells Luke that he must enter a cave made from the roots of a tree, a mystic cave that is strong with the dark side of the Force, Luke asks his new mentor what lies within. "Only what you take with you," Yoda replies. Ignoring Yoda's request, Luke straps on his weapons and enters the cave. There he encounters Darth Vader, or what appears to be Vader. For as Luke strikes out with his lightsaber, his opponent's head falls off—only to reveal the face of Luke inside Vader's helmet. "This is truly a descent into another spiritual labyrinth, for in the depths of the tree lies the revelation that Darth Vader is not some external evil presence but the shadow side of Luke himself," Henderson notes. "The dark side of the Force lies within as well as without." Luke is again confronted with the inescapable when he finally encounters Vader in the bowels of Cloud City and is told the horrible truth: Vader is no evil stranger; Luke is his own flesh and blood.

Finally, in *Return of the Jedi,* Luke realizes that the only way to resolve the crisis is to again confront his father. He surrenders to him, is taken before the utterly irredeemable Emperor Palpatine, and eventually is goaded into attacking Vader. After Luke severs his father's bionic hand, he looks at his own electro-mechanical hand and realizes that if he missteps, he could become the next Darth Vader. When the Emperor then starts to destroy Luke, son appeals to father for help. At the last possible moment, Vader manages to cast off years of dark-side regimentation and kills the Emperor to save his son. "Vader has detached himself from his evil master and has been transformed through his son," Henderson notes. "Vader has become a tragic persona, and his own suffering is now the supreme monstrosity with which he must contend. . . . Vader is, in a sense, a fallen angel who reveals his true essence at last."

II: THE SAGA
OF DARTH VADER

Anakin Skywalker was many things in his tormented and antithetical life: hero and tyrant, father and murderer. Like a near-mythic figure out of an ancient Jedi Holocron, Anakin lived on an epic scale few beings can fully comprehend. His actions had more influence, for both good and ill, than just about any other individual in galactic history. Under the name of Darth Vader he was responsible for some of the most brutal atrocities in the annals of the galaxy, yet it was his final act of heroism that cut the malignant heart out of the amoral Empire. Though many survivors of Vader's cruelty are reluctant to forgive him his crimes, the legendary Jedi appears to have found peace beyond death in the radiant energy of the Force.

Historians are just beginning to uncover details of Anakin's early life, since numerous archives were destroyed during the Galactic Civil War. Furthermore, when Anakin assumed the mantle of Darth Vader he attempted to stamp out all vestiges of his former existence.

One fact not in dispute is that young Anakin Skywalker was trained as a Jedi by Obi-Wan Kenobi. Anakin, tempted by the dark side of the Force, coldly turned his back on those he loved. A chastened Kenobi desperately tried to bring his pupil back from the self-destructive course he had chosen, but Anakin would not be swayed. They had a confrontation that was both awe-inspiring and terrifying and from which Anakin emerged a broken man.

Horribly disfigured on the outside, Anakin's internal injuries were so severe that he was no longer able to survive without extensive bio-machinery to keep his damaged heart pumping and his ruined lungs inflated. He was forced to encase himself in a full-body armored suit, a walking coffin of blinking pulmonary regulators and hissing oxygen intakes. Never again would Anakin be able to live life as normal

men did; he was now a nightmare in black, glaring out at the world through the dark lenses of his grotesque demonic countenance. From that moment, Anakin Skywalker became Darth Vader in appearance as well as in spirit. The latest Dark Lord of the Sith built a lightsaber with a blood-red blade to replace his former blue sword and all but hid the weapon's shining silver handle beneath a suffocating sheath of black grips. Consumed with anger and hatred, Vader went on to a new life in the corrupt service of Palpatine.

Twin children—a boy and a girl—were Anakin's unseen legacy. Obi-Wan helped conceal the infants from their father's attention and the Emperor's depredations, hoping that one day the Skywalker offspring would rise to challenge the tyranny of evil. Darth Vader, meanwhile, helped his master solidify his claim to the title of Galactic Emperor by hunting down and exterminating the surviving Jedi Knights. As his control over the dark side deepened, Vader grew increasingly contemptuous of his previous life as a mere student. The Dark Lord possessed immeasurable power and unquestionable authority. He knelt before the Emperor and no one else.

Only by sealing himself in a hyperbaric medical chamber could Vader peel away his desensitizing body plating, and then only for a short time. He was determined to use the energies of the dark side to one day heal his shattered body and shed his armor forever. Vader's failure at this task only intensified his rage.

As time ground on and Palpatine's unyielding grip expanded, politicians such as Bail Organa and Mon Mothma asserted their dissident views on the floor of the Imperial Senate. Before long, an insurgent movement dedicated to the Emperor's overthrow began taking shape. In Vader's eyes, such a development was unpredictable and potentially dangerous. Palpatine agreed, and permitted Grand Moff Tarkin

to build a gargantuan Imperial terror weapon with the ominous code name Death Star. One of the battle station's first targets would be the hidden military base that the Rebels had established on an as-yet undetermined world.

Construction began, but the war against the Rebel Alliance intensified as more planets summoned the courage to speak out against official Imperial doctrine. The Emperor dispatched his Star Destroyers to deal with the growing problem in a brutal and heavy-handed fashion. Lord Vader watched the latest suppression with indifference. Enemies of the Empire deserved whatever gruesome deaths Palpatine saw fit to mete out, but the whole campaign would ultimately amount to little more than the stamping out of insignificant brushfires. The Force was what truly mattered, the exhilarating and at times frightening ability to manipulate life itself and to bend the very structure of reality. Still, the Grand Moff's new toy was swiftly nearing completion above Despayre, helped along by the Dark Lord's terrifying motivational techniques. Despite the weapon's gross size and exorbitant cost, Vader admitted it could make an excellent deterrent in the short run.

Due to the increase in military activity, Palpatine grew more reliant on Darth Vader to act as his eyes and ears among his Imperial subjects. Even the Emperor's most straightforward requests hid covert plots and secret agendas; Palpatine's true reasons for sending his servant off on minor administrative inspections were a mystery to Vader. Would Palpatine move against him in his absence? Was the Falleen prince Xizor, head of the galaxy's largest criminal syndicate, becoming the Emperor's most trusted confidant? Did Palpatine suspect that Vader had sometimes entertained the thought of overthrowing his master and assuming the throne in his place? But Vader was in no position to criticize or even raise the question. On his master's orders, he left Imperial City on Coruscant, now called Imperial Center, to oversee Lord Tion's subjugation of the rebellious planet Ralltiir.

10000011110010100011101101111011010101010101001001010101101101000100001010100101010010100101010101001001010010100101

1101000001111001010001110110111101101010101010101010010010

Vader's *Lambda*-class shuttle bypassed Ralltiir's planetary fleet blockade and landed without ceremony on the devastated sphere. Once one of the most respected members of the Core Worlds, the planet now seethed with white-armored stormtroopers and black-clad Imperial inquisitors. The Dark Lord immediately sought out Tion and let the pompous fool know that the Emperor was watching his every move. He then left to inspect the central interrogation camp.

In Vader's absence, another ship joined his shuttle on the landing pad. The *Tantive IV*, a Blockade Runner of the Royal House of Alderaan, had arrived on a "mercy mission" carrying medical supplies and spare parts. The vessel's chief passenger was none other than Princess Leia Organa, the young rabble-rousing politician who had recently electrified the Imperial Senate with her firebrand rhetoric. Darth Vader learned of her arrival at the same moment that Ralltiir insurgents attacked the spaceport's southern perimeter, a diversion, Vader was sure. The Dark Lord rushed back to the landing pad and engaged the Princess in some verbal sparring but left her and her ship unharmed.

Unbeknownst to Vader, Leia escaped from Ralltiir with a wounded Rebel soldier who had information about the Death Star's construction. Alerted to the superweapon's existence, the Alliance put every effort into derailing the project. A subsequent attack on a space convoy traveling from Eriadu to the Imperial vaults resulted in the capture of most of the battle station's schematics; more blueprints were stolen by a Rebel agent from a research facility on Danuta. When the two sets of plans were combined, they formed a complete technical readout of the Death Star including its defensive vulnerabilities and structural weaknesses. Princess Leia left in the *Tantive IV* to intercept this stolen data from a Rebel cell on Toprawa.

The Emperor's spies learned that something significant would soon happen at Toprawa, and Darth Vader was sent to shut it down. Aboard the Imperial Star Destroyer *Devastator*, the Sith Lord monitored the

000111010011101000001111001010001110110111101101010101010100100100101010101011010100100100001010100101001010
010101001010010100101001000100101000100111001011001000

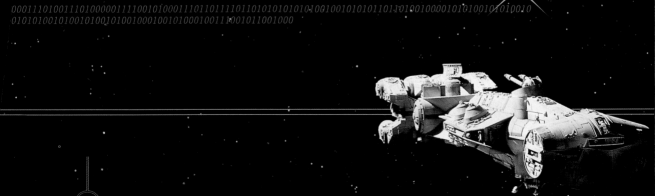

reports filtering in from his ground troops, who were assaulting a fortified Rebel position on Toprawa's surface. The lead squad seemed close to victory but Vader ordered his three auxiliary Star Destroyers to assume close planetary orbit in case a surface bombardment became necessary. As the last of the prodigious vessels slid into position, the *Tantive IV* emerged from hyperspace.

The Blockade Runner claimed to be experiencing a malfunction, but Vader was no fool. The *Devastator*'s captain ordered the consular ship to heave to and prepare to receive Imperial investigators. As the vast Star Destroyer closed with the much smaller vessel, an officer in the crew pit confirmed Vader's suspicions: the *Tantive IV* had downloaded a coded, high-burst data transmission beamed from the Rebel facility on Toprawa. They had the Death Star plans, Vader knew. They must not be allowed to escape! The *Devastator* opened fire.

As the gunners poured scarlet energy at their target, the Blockade Runner lurched forward and vanished into hyperspace with a tiny wink of triumph. Several officers on the bridge gasped. Darth Vader's cold-blooded capriciousness in executing those who had displeased him was legendary. But Vader had an alternate method for locating and tracking his fugitive quarry. Imperial Intelligence had placed a spy aboard the *Tantive IV*, a protocol droid designated U-3PO. The Star Destroyer followed the droid's unerring homing signal through the twists of hyperspace, and when the Blockade Runner reverted back into realspace at the brown orb of Tatooine, the *Devastator* leapt out nearly on top of it.

The small ship was taken by surprise. A desperate, furious exchange of energy bolts ended when the *Devastator*'s turbolasers hit the Blockade Runner's main solar fin. Crippled beyond repair, the *Tantive IV* shut down its main reactor and was helplessly dragged into the Star Destroyer's yawning hangar bay.

Foolishly, the ship still refused to surrender and receive boarders. Vader clenched his fist with rage. Very well then; their fates would be on their own heads. The Sith Lord assembled an assault squad of his finest

shock troops and ordered them through a blaster-chewed hull breach. Once the firing died down, he followed them into the swirling smoke.

Shots echoed along the corridor walls as Vader strode through the passenger decks. He had no fear for his personal safety. As a Dark Lord of the Sith he was capable of deflecting blaster bolts with nothing more than an outstretched palm. Vader soon located the captain, an average-stock Alderaanian named Antilles. Though a telekinetic choke was an excellent method of sharpening the Force's effect on physical matter, sometimes a simple one-handed squeeze could loosen recalcitrant tongues more quickly.

"Where are those transmissions you intercepted?" growled Vader. **"What have you done with those plans?"** The Rebel clung to his cover story of being on a diplomatic mission, and his life ended with a gurgling death rattle. Behind his mask, Vader's jaw clenched in anger. There could be as many as one hundred sixty-five crewmen aboard a vessel of this size. If he had to interrogate them all, so be it.

In less time than he had expected, his stormtroopers brought forth Leia Organa. Vader made it a point to remind the young captive of their recent meeting on Ralltiir. **"You weren't on any mercy mission this time,"** he said. **"Several transmissions were beamed to this ship by Rebel spies."** The Princess, like the captain before her, reiterated the story that the *Tantive IV* was a mere consular ship on official diplomatic business. **"You are part of the Rebel Alliance and a traitor!"** Vader proclaimed. **"Take her away!"**

The Princess was transferred to a detention cell aboard the *Devastator*. Vader ordered his officers to transmit a broadband distress signal from the *Tantive IV*'s bridge computer and then inform the Imperial Senate, with much regret, that all the ship's passengers had been killed in a mishap. Commander Praji appeared and delivered an update on the search for the Death Star plans. "Lord Vader," he reported, "the battle station plans are not on board this ship. An escape pod was jettisoned during the

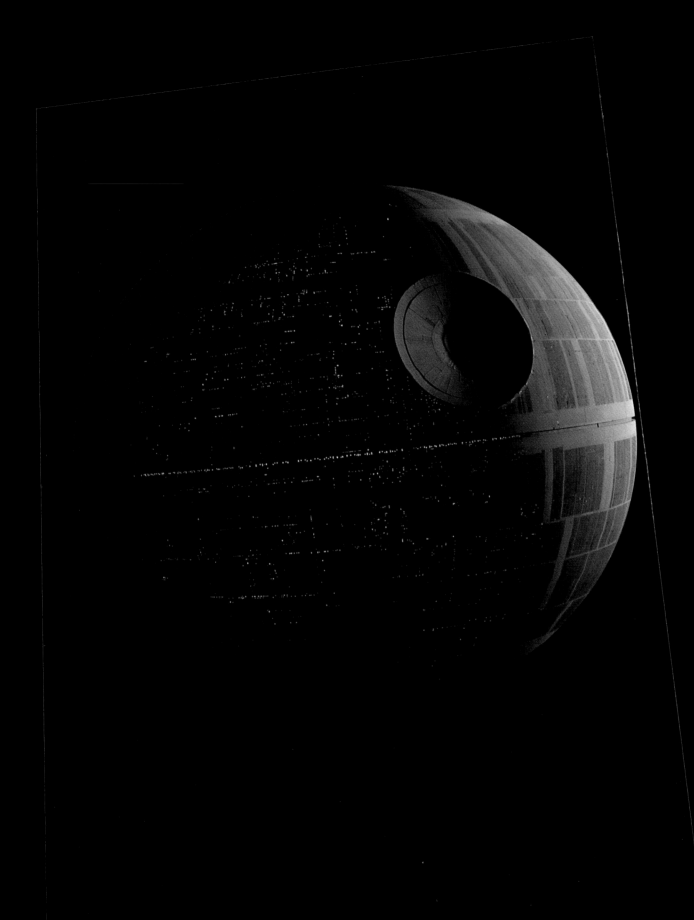

fighting, but no life signs were aboard." Vader sensed that the plans were indeed aboard the pod. **"Send a detachment down to retrieve it,"** Vader ordered. **"See to it *personally*, Commander. There'll be no one to stop us this time!"**

The *Devastator*'s hyperspace transit from Tatooine to the Death Star was smooth and uneventful. Vader stood confidently on the command deck as the Star Destroyer approached the battle station and passed through its concentric rings of invisible defensive zones. On a whim he had Princess Leia brought to the bridge, where he showed her the Empire's man-made moon, a swollen gray sphere packing enough destructive energy to shatter a planet like an ornamented crystal globe. It was a mere machine in Vader's eyes, but it was indicative of the Empire's galaxy-spanning might. The sight of the weapon frightened and disturbed Leia but did not prod her into revealing what she had done with the intercepted technical readouts. Vader gave her one last chance to reveal what she knew before they arrived. Once imprisoned in the Death Star's interrogation block, more persuasive methods would be applied. The defiant senator stubbornly refused to reveal any information.

Grand Moff Tarkin met Vader in the Death Star's docking bay. The Dark Lord held a certain degree of respect for the gaunt Imperial governor, and he knew Tarkin felt the same way about him. But neither man liked or trusted the other. Tarkin resented having Palpatine's personal hatchet man peering over his shoulder, and Vader suspected that the Grand Moff was plotting to use his new superweapon to achieve unprecedented power in the Empire, possibly even to overthrow the Emperor himself. The fact that Vader harbored similar ambitions only deepened his wary suspicion.

Stepping into a turbolift, the two men exchanged a few terse words as they arrived at the Death Star's administrative conference room on the command level. Twin ebony doors hissed open, revealing a circular table and roughly a dozen chairs in which the galaxy's top military officers sat attentively. General

1001110110111101101010101010101001001010101011011010010000101010101010101001011000100101001010101001

Tagge and Admiral Motti were spitting angry words at one another as they entered, but both stopped to regard Tarkin and his black-armored escort. The Grand Moff took his seat and informed the group of the Emperor's recent dissolution of the Imperial Senate.

Vader remained standing, watching as emotions of shock, greed, and ambition played across the assembled faces. Admiral Motti in particular appeared to despise his presence; waves of contempt emanated from his body. Soon enough, the arrogant officer spoke his mind. "Don't try to frighten us with your sorcerer's ways, Lord Vader," he began. More insolent words tumbled from his mouth before Vader reached out with invisible Force tendrils and neatly pinched his windpipe. The admiral sputtered and began turning a fine shade of blue before Tarkin spoke up. "Enough of this. Vader, release him!" The Dark Lord paused and allowed sarcasm to seep into his voice. **"As you wish."** He gestured with one gloved hand and Motti slumped forward, chastised and humiliated.

Darth Vader had other, more important business to attend to in the detention block. As he entered Cell 2187 accompanied by two guards and a robotic IT-O Interrogator, the captured Princess shrank back. The hovering torture droid seemed to fill the tiny room. Vader spoke with cold, measured words. **"And now, Your Highness, we will discuss the location of your hidden Rebel base."** The droid injected Leia with a mixture of serums, sending her into a hypnotic trance. But the Dark Lord's best efforts, including psychological manipulation and Force probing, amounted to nothing. The senator's inner fortitude was baffling and unexpected. For lack of a better explanation, Vader attributed it to the mental training received by all members of the House of Alderaan.

The Grand Moff proposed another path. A threat to a third party could often overcome the most resolute resistance, and nothing was more dear to Leia than her homeworld of Alderaan. Vader initially objected

to such an ambitious scheme. Alderaan was one of the most respected Core Worlds, and Tarkin had neglected to consult the Emperor on his decision, but he finally conceded. The destruction of Alderaan would eliminate a hotbed of Rebel sentiment and demonstrate to the galaxy that the Empire had an unstoppable weapon at its disposal.

The Death Star made a hyperspace jump to Alderaan and hung there in space above the placid blue orb. The Princess was escorted to the overbridge. An immense wall screen displayed their target, and Tarkin did his best to impress upon his captive the dire fate awaiting her world if she continued to refuse to reveal the site of the Rebel base. Finally, she broke down. "Dantooine," the Princess said. "They're on Dantooine." Tarkin turned toward Vader with a small twinkle of triumph in his eyes. "You see, Lord Vader, she can be reasonable. Continue with the operation. You may fire when ready." Leia was aghast as the superlaser gunners began their awesome task; the deck plates began to thrum with a mammoth surge of pent-up energy, and in one shattering instant, an entire world became nothing but pulverized rubble.

Vader later met with Tarkin in the conference room to discuss their next course of action. The Sith Lord could still sense the voices of the Alderaanian dead, a distant after-echo swirling in the Force as a turbulent vortex of agony. He put such thoughts aside. With Alderaan demolished and Dantooine next on the list, the two largest centers of resistance to Imperial rule would no longer be a factor. Imperial scout ships, however, brought back unexpected news. Dantooine was nothing but a ruse. Enraged, Tarkin ordered the Princess' immediate execution.

As the Death Star made plans to depart the Alderaan system, the crew reported that it had captured an arriving space freighter, one that appeared to be the same ship that had outrun a Star Destroyer patrol at

Tatooine. Darth Vader personally looked over the dilapidated pirate craft and sensed . . . *something*—a strange vibration in the Force, a unique sensation he hadn't encountered in years. Vader left the docking bay, but the more he thought about his experience the more certain he became of its root cause. Obi-Wan Kenobi had returned.

Tarkin was predictably skeptical. "The Jedi are extinct," he said. "Their fire has gone out of the universe. You, my friend, are all that's left of their religion." As if on cue, the comlink buzzed with an urgent report of a disturbance in the Princess' cell bay. **"Obi-Wan is here,"** Vader said. **"The Force is with him."**

The Force drew the two Jedi toward their inevitable confrontation. Neither expressed surprise when they encountered one another in the stark corridor outside Bay 327. **"I've been waiting for you, Obi-Wan,"** intoned the fallen pupil. **"We meet again at last. When I left you I was but the learner; now I am the master."** The two moved in a careful circle, striking and parrying. Lightsabers moaned and flashed as the two former friends took stock of what each had become over the years. "You can't win, Darth," warned Obi-Wan. "If you strike me down I shall become more powerful than you can possibly imagine."

They continued to exchange blows, and the other members of Kenobi's party ran into the docking bay towards the *Falcon*'s open ramp. Obi-Wan shifted his eyes toward them and seemed to reach a decision. Drawing an aura of Force around his aged form, he raised his saber in a passive salute. Vader, with a mighty sweep of his crimson blade, cleaved his former master in two.

But Kenobi's robes fluttered to the deck, empty. Vader poked at them with one black boot. Then he turned his attention toward the pirate freighter and strode ahead, saber in hand. A closing blast door pre-

vented his forward passage. The armored panes of durasteel made little difference to one who had the Force. Vader could feel the freighter powering up, as it rocketed away from the Death Star with Leia on board. The Dark Lord smiled, switched off his saber, and bent down to retrieve Obi-Wan's fallen weapon from the crumpled pile of brown cloth. A fine trophy, and a fitting one. He would have it transferred immediately to his private fortress on Vjun. The torch had been passed.

A short time later, he stood with Tarkin on the battle station's overbridge. The Grand Moff expressed understandable concern about the wisdom of Vader's plan. The Death Star could easily have rotated and brought another tractor-beam projector to bear on the fleeing ship; intentionally allowing the vessel to escape could prove to be a career-ending debacle. Vader, however, was serenely confident. The homing beacon placed onboard would lead them to the Rebel base, and their ultimate triumph would follow soon after. It would not be long now.

With a shudder, the titanic Death Star emerged from hyperspace in the Yavin system. Engineers and navigators on the overbridge began shouting out numbers as positioning data began to fill their monitor screens. The Rebel base was on a jungle moon on the opposite side of the immense planet Yavin. If the battle station executed a simple orbit around the orange gas giant at maximum sublight speed, in just over thirty minutes they would have a clean shot at the Rebels' den.

Darth Vader watched the proceedings with satisfaction. **"This will be a day long remembered,"** he told Tarkin. **"It has seen the end of Kenobi; it will soon see the end of the Rebellion."** The Grand Moff seemed indifferent, absorbed in the intricate workings of his so-called ultimate weapon. Vader took his leave of the governor, ostensibly to make a personal inspection tour of the battle station's defenses. In reality, he wanted to get away from the machinations of Tarkin and his scheming subordinate, Admiral Motti.

ANAKIN SKYWALKER: THE STORY OF DARTH VADER

010101010010010101011011010010000101010010101010010100101010101001010010100101

It wasn't long before the Rebels launched their counterattack with a ragged flight group of anti-quated Y-wing fighters and the newer Incom T-65 X-wings. Vader watched the enemy's battle plan with interest. The tiny snubfighters appeared maneuverable enough to slip unmolested through the battle station's defensive screen, which hadn't been designed to repel anything smaller than a capital ship assault. Tarkin might be arrogant enough to dismiss the Rebel threat, but the Dark Lord had learned never to underestimate an opponent. **"We'll have to destroy them ship-to-ship,"** he ordered. **"Get the crews to their fighters."**

A squadron of TIEs soon joined the Rebel raiders, swooping and diving in a succession of vicious dogfights. Vader stayed near a tactical station and monitored the unfolding action. He doubted that this was a mere suicide attack, and the random collateral damage to the Death Star's superstructure could easily serve as cover for a more targeted strike. Within moments, he saw three Y-wings streak away from the fray and head straight for one of the many surface trenches. Vader summoned his personal wingmen, who stood ready for flight in their black pilot vacsuits. **"Several fighters have broken off from the main group,"** he informed them. **"Come with me."** The hangar was just a short distance away; his custom fighter hung from the overhead rack in the coveted front launch position. The unique vessel, a hyperdrive-equipped prototype, sported a radical bent-winged configuration that brought to mind a dark fist clenched in anger. His wingmen's standard-model TIEs, designated Black 2 and Black 3, dangled on either side. Within minutes, the three expert pilots were soaring through the vacuum of space.

The Y-wings were easy to locate and even easier to reach; the twin ion engines of a TIE fighter were capable of remarkable sublight speed. In the narrow confines of the trench, the Rebel ships would have no chance of avoiding their lasers. **"I'll take them myself,"** Vader told his wingmen. **"Cover me."** The Rebel ships went down easily: one, two, three.

Vader and his escorts peeled away from the Death Star's surface. Y-wings were slow and ungainly, but they made excellent precision bombers; Vader expected the Rebels to send more of that particular craft back into the trench. Surprisingly, a group of three X-wing fighters took their place. The better-armed X-wings were faster and presented their own set of challenges. Vader slipped his deadly TIE back into the trench. He enjoyed a challenge.

Instead of clustering together in a tight formation, two fighters were holding back to cover the lead starfighter with their quad lasers. Vader destroyed the two rear vessels, then kicked his throttle up to full to catch the front ship before it could fire its proton torpedoes. He didn't make it. The X-wing loosed a twin volley of destructive energy, engulfing the end of the trench in a billow of flame, plasma, and superheated metal. Vader roared through the expanding cloud and kept his instruments trained on the fleeing Rebel. Within moments, he had scored another kill.

Black 2 and Black 3 followed the Sith Lord as he swung around for another pass. The proton torpedoes did not appear to have caused serious damage. Vader dropped into position behind another group of three X-wings rocketing through the trench at top speed. He made an adjustment to his fighter's energy management settings and shunted increased power to the engines.

One X-wing took a minor hit and started to lose speed. Moments later, it shot out of the plasteel furrow and climbed for the stars. **"Let him go,"** Vader ordered his wingmen. **"Stay on the leader."** The second X-wing escort exploded in a brilliant fireball. Just one ship remained.

As Vader neared the breakneck fugitive, he sensed a strange aura emanating from the ship's pilot. Force-sensitive, of that he was sure, but there was more to it than that. It was almost as if he could feel the presence of Obi-Wan Kenobi himself. **"The Force is strong in this one,"** he muttered aloud.

1101001110100011010010000101010010101010010100101010100101001010010101001000
01000100101000100111001011001000110001110100111010000011110010100000011111

1101101

Vader was having a difficult time getting a targeting lock. Frustrated, he snapped off a few ranging shots, one of which hit the head of the X-wing's astromech unit. Smoke boiled from the damaged droid and the TIEs moved closer. Vader checked his computer readout. The X-wing's silhouette jumped to the center of the targeting box, and a high-pitched warbling tone indicated a weapons lock. **"I have you now!"**

In an instant, all the forces of chaos broke loose. Black 3 burst into a million incandescent fragments that continued to race down the trench through the force of inertia. Vader jerked his head upward. **"What?!"** A huge vessel was barreling down on their position straight from the direction of Yavin's sun. Black 2 panicked, throwing his control yoke to the right and bouncing off Vader's port solar panel before hitting the side wall. Thrown off balance, Vader's TIE spun crazily into space as its pilot struggled vainly with the maneuvering thrusters.

In the next few seconds, the phototropic canopy of the TIE fighter darkened in response to a colossal supernova of released energy, and the small craft bucked savagely in the tumultuous shockwave. Vader felt more than a million lives extinguish with a distant scream of futility. The most destructive weapon in the galaxy—the Grand Moff's technological terror—had been destroyed.

It took some time for Vader to reach Imperial space in his damaged fighter. He returned to find turmoil. Many of the best and brightest officers had been killed at Yavin, including Grand Moff Tarkin, and the Rebel Alliance had been handed a gift-wrapped propaganda victory. Remaining Imperial officers were either jockeying for position in the new hierarchy or pointing fingers to lay blame for the Death Star fiasco.

Darth Vader started preparing a second move against the Rebel base, this time with an unstoppable Imperial fleet instead of an untested doomsday weapon. An arrogant but competent officer named

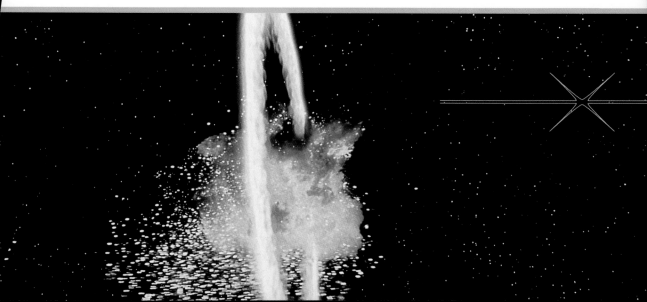

Admiral Griff executed a blockade of the Yavin system, placing Interdictor cruisers along the major hyperspace routes and preventing any of the Rebel high command from evacuating their jungle moon. But Vader refused to give him permission to strike. The first Super Star Destroyer ever constructed would soon be launched from the shipyards at Fondor and Palpatine had promised his servant that the colossal vessel would be his. Vader vowed to wipe the Rebel scourge from the surface of the Yavin moon with the formidable new flagship as his death-dealing chariot.

As the warship neared completion the Dark Lord busied himself. The torture of a captured Rebel soldier revealed the astounding name of the pilot who had seemed so strong in the Force during the final trench run: Skywalker. Deep inside the black metallic shell, a flicker of joy came to life—it had to be his son. Just as quickly, darkness closed around the flame. His son was on the side that had to be destroyed.

Several Imperial admirals, incensed over the Sith Lord's delay of the Yavin attack, moved against Vader on Fondor but were outsmarted. On Aridus, Vader set a trap that showed artful promise but failed to ensnare the Skywalker boy. Before long, he took command of the finished Super Star Destroyer, newly christened *Executor*, and headed for Yavin to crush the base into blackened dust.

But the Rebels had thrown together a hasty evacuation. And Admiral Griff grievously miscalculated a hyperspace microjump and collided with the *Executor*, allowing the Rebel withdrawal force to leap to hyperspace.

The Rebels could now be anywhere in the galaxy; the search for them would be lengthy and tiresome. Darth Vader led the hunt from the bridge of the *Executor*, running down leads on Jazbina and other scattered worlds. A call from an Imperial regional governor named Bin Essada touched off one of the most aggravating encounters.

Essada relayed a report from Mimban, a sodden, forsaken mudpit in the Circarpous system. The planet's Imperial overseer had somehow bungled his way into capturing Luke Skywalker and Princess Leia Organa but was too stupid to realize his prisoners' true identities. Darth Vader arrived at the world to take the pair into custody, but they had already escaped into the trackless swamps. With help from a crystalline shard that appeared to focus and magnify the Force, Vader tracked the fugitives to a vine-encrusted temple ruin and defeated the Princess in elementary lightsaber combat.

The boy proved much more of a challenge. He was reluctant to admit it, but the presence of Obi-Wan Kenobi clung to the youth like a second skin and seemed to be guiding his precocious actions. In a final burst of screaming energy, Luke's saber blade sliced through the Dark Lord's right arm where the limb met the shoulder. Vader reeled from the blow but quickly regained his focus; he could sense that Kenobi's essence had vanished and would not be able to move against him again. As he stepped forward to claim his exhausted prize, a single misstep sent him plunging down a crumbling stone well. In the time it took Vader to extract himself, both Rebels had abandoned the temple.

As the Civil War intensified, the Imperials scored a few propaganda victories, including a devastating strike against a supply convoy at Derra IV that cost the Rebels dearly. Buoyed by the recent string of successes, Lord Vader's elite Death Squadron—five Star Destroyers led by the command ship *Executor*—continued to search for the new Rebel base. Captain Needa and the *Avenger* were in charge of releasing Arakyd probe droids that rocketed off in one-way hyperspace pods to the farthest reaches of the Outer Rim Territories.

Unbeknownst to his subordinates, Vader harbored a more personal agenda that went hand-in-hand with his stated goal of crushing the Rebels. Ever since he had learned the name of the X-wing pilot who had

destroyed the Death Star, he had obsessed over the possibility that Luke Skywalker—his son—could be persuaded to stand by his side and learn the secrets of the dark side of the Force. The Skywalker blood ran hot. Young Luke held great power and limitless potential; his raw strength even exceeded Vader's own. Together, no one could oppose them, not even the Emperor.

During moments of quiet meditation in his hyperbaric chamber, Vader received insights, seemingly from the Force, into his son's whereabouts. Perhaps it was destiny that the two should meet again. After one meditation session, the Dark Lord contacted the *Avenger*'s crew and ordered them to launch probe droids at the frozen planets Allyuen, Tokmia, and Hoth.

When Captain Piett reported an intriguing probe droid transmission to Admiral Ozzel, the superior officer on the *Executor* upbraided him about the sketchy quality of the information. Vader cut them off. **"You found something?"** he growled. Piett seemed pleased to have a sympathetic ear and gestured toward the image on the monitor screen transmitted from a frigid world ostensibly empty of intelligent life: a half-buried planetary shield generator.

"That's it," boomed Vader. **"The Rebels are there."** Ozzel's annoyance at having his authority publicly countermanded gave the Dark Lord a small twinge of pleasure.

The fleet left immediately for the Hoth system and Darth Vader retired to his meditation chamber for the final leg of the journey. His quiet contemplation was interrupted by General Veers, who informed him that the Death Squadron had successfully dropped from hyperspace but encountered an impenetrable defensive energy shield on the system's sixth planet. Vader was livid. Ozzel had bungled the emergence from hyperspace and tipped their hand. **"He is as clumsy as he is stupid,"** fumed the Sith Lord, who told Veers to prepare his All Terrain Armored Transport battalions for the inevitable fight.

Behind Vader an enormous viewscreen flickered to life, displaying the *Executor*'s bridge. Ozzel turned to regard the Dark Lord and smoothly launched into an update on the fleet's current status. His self-assured words suddenly caught in his throat. **"You have failed me for the last time, Admiral,"** growled Vader, imperceptibly reaching through the transmission screen and squeezing Ozzel's neck in an unbending vise. As the former commander of his fleet labored desperately for oxygen, Vader summoned Captain Piett to the fore. The bright and ambitious officer listened carefully to the battle instructions. **"Make ready to land our troops beyond the energy shield and deploy the fleet so that nothing gets off that system. You are in command now, *Admiral* Piett!"** A shadow of worry crossed Piett's lined face as Ozzel fell to the deck with a loud thump.

The Battle of Hoth was a one-sided slaughter. The ineffectual Rebel counterattack only delayed the inevitable; hundreds of their troops perished and millions of credits worth of heavy equipment, including an extraordinarily expensive KDY Planet Defender ion cannon, were abandoned or destroyed. Even so, a handful of transports and X-wing fighters were able to slip through the Star Destroyer blockade and most of the Rebel command staff managed to avoid capture. More troublesome in Vader's eyes, Luke Skywalker and the smuggling ship he often traveled with, the *Millennium Falcon,* were both missing. The latter was particularly vexing, as Vader had entered the hollowed-out Rebel snow hangar just in time to see the battered freighter blast off into the icy blue sky.

Darth Vader returned to the *Executor* to monitor the ongoing pursuit. Soon, he had welcome news: the *Millennium Falcon* had been sighted. A knot of TIE fighters and several massive Star Destroyers engaged the fugitive freighter, and based on their tactical analysis, reported that the vessel did not appear to have a working hyperdrive. Interrupting the Sith Lord's private meditation session in the hyperbaric chamber, newly appointed Admiral Piett saw the immutable black helmet suspended high in the air between a set of mechanical jaws. Vader sensed the mix of respect and repugnance play over Piett's face as he waited

until the veined, scarred horror that was Vader's head was safely covered before speaking. "Our ships have sighted the *Millennium Falcon,*" Piett began. "But it has entered an asteroid field and we cannot risk. . . ." **"Asteroids do not concern me,"** Vader interrupted. **"I want that ship."** The fate of his predecessor still fresh in his mind, the admiral hurried to obey.

All Star Destroyers, including the *Executor,* were diverted into the swirling asteroid storm. Turbolaser gunners blasted the largest rocks; those they missed impacted against the bow shields like multi-megaton compression bombs. Structural damage and incidental casualties were mounting. Via a holographic communications link, Captain Needa tried to impress upon his liege the futility of their self-destructive search. "Considering the amount of damage we've sustained, they must have been destroyed." Darth Vader would have none of it. He could sense an intangible essence among the asteroids. At that moment, Admiral Piett came forward with some startling information: the Emperor was waiting to speak with him on his personal HoloNet linkup.

Palpatine's communications to the fleet were infrequent but could never be ignored. After ordering Piett to head out of the enshrouding asteroid swarm, Vader hurried to the *Executor*'s communications vault. He knelt with humble obedience, his servile presence activating the oversized hologram of the galaxy's cruel overlord. Palpatine's eyes burned like smoldering embers from his shriveled and age-ravaged face. "There is a great disturbance in the Force," the apparition began, its voice dark and sepulchral. "We have a new enemy: Luke Skywalker." Vader listened with secret apprehension. He knew his master wanted Skywalker dead, but Vader had plans for his long-absent son, if he could just convince Palpatine to keep Skywalker alive. **"He's just a boy,"** he began, but the Emperor stubbornly reminded him of Luke's untapped power. Vader persisted. **"If he could be turned, he would become a powerful ally,"** he offered hopefully. The Emperor considered the matter for a moment. "Yes," he said finally. "Yes. He would be a great asset. Can it be done?" Vader smiled inwardly over his private victory. **"He will join us or die, my master."**

The capture of the *Millennium Falcon* was now more important than ever. The Dark Lord possessed valued contacts among all strata of galactic society; by calling on a few of the more disreputable, he had quickly assembled on the *Executor*'s bridge six of the deadliest bounty hunters: Bossk, Dengar, IG-88, Zuckuss, 4-LOM, and of course, Boba Fett. Their presence on his flagship sent a public message to his officers that they had failed in their assigned duties. Vader made his demands clear to the hunters, taking special care to emphasize that only a live delivery would be accepted. Before he could finish, Piett, with relief evident on his face, interrupted to report that the Star Destroyer *Avenger* had located their elusive quarry. With muttered curses, the bounty hunters scattered to their ships.

The *Avenger*'s pursuit was fast and fruitless. One moment Captain Needa was confidently predicting a smooth capture; the next moment he was admitting that the *Falcon* had vanished into thin air. His desire to publicly apologize saved Vader the trouble of seeking him out, but the end result was the same. Two guards dragged Needa's cooling corpse from its supine position on the *Executor*'s smooth deckplates as Vader turned to listen to Piett's bleak status report. The admiral confessed that the Imperial fleet had found nothing, and that the surprisingly slippery *Falcon* could now be almost anywhere in the vastness of interstellar space. **"Alert all commands,"** he barked. **"Calculate every possible destination along their last known trajectory. Don't fail me again, Admiral!"**

The Sith Lord's unorthodox tactic of hiring free-lance bounty hunters paid off where polished military precision had not. It was Boba Fett who contacted Vader, announcing he had located the *Falcon* and tracked its likely destination to Cloud City in the nearby Bespin system. The *Executor* and Fett's *Slave I* arrived at the floating metropolis before the Rebels' damaged vessel could, and Vader immediately summoned the local ruling council. Cloud City's baron-administrator, a charismatic man named Lando Calrissian, was clearly opposed to dealing with the Empire. But several columns of marching stormtroopers made it clear that he had little choice. Up until now the city's gas-mining operation had escaped direct

Imperial control; by exploiting the baron's hopes that the Super Star Destroyer would simply leave after capturing its prey, Vader could play him like a set of nalargon pipes.

The stormtroopers were secreted behind blast doors and the *Executor* was sent to the far side of Bespin as the *Millennium Falcon* touched down on landing platform 327. Calrissian played his role perfectly, greeting Han Solo in the exuberant fashion expected between two long-separated comrades and gaining the wary trust of Princess Leia, her protocol droid, and Solo's Wookiee co-pilot, Chewbacca. One trooper nearly spoiled the ambush by blasting the over-inquisitive C-3PO when he wandered down a side avenue, but the total damage was minimal. The Rebels would be irrevocably ensnared before they could realize anything was seriously amiss.

Vader reconnected with Boba Fett and the two men waited for their targets in Cloud City's most opulent banquet hall. Right on time, Calrissian escorted his guests to the entrance. The door hissed open, the Wookiee howled, and the Princess froze in stunned horror. With admirable reflexes, the Corellian pirate pulled his blaster and snapped off several shots that would have hit dead center on Vader's chest controls. Instead, the energy projectiles burned harmlessly into the walls as Vader deflected them with one outstretched hand. A simple pull on the fabric of the Force sent Solo's weapon flying across the laden table and into his waiting palm. **"We would be honored if you would join us,"** said Vader smugly. Boba Fett took up position next to him and a squad of stormtroopers blocked the only exit. The bait was secure; now only Skywalker remained.

The bond between Luke and his friends was strong. If his son possessed half the Force potential that Vader suspected, he would detect his comrades' plight across light-years of uncharted galactic space and rush heedlessly to rescue them. To be on the safe side, Vader decided to ensure that the feelings thrown off by Leia, Han, and the Wookiee were particularly *acute*.

A program of torture, starvation, and sensory deprivation followed, with Solo bearing the brunt of the agony. Perhaps an extended session on a bed of electro-prods would teach the Corellian to never again cross weapons with a Lord of the Sith. As screams reverberated through the interrogation chamber, Vader exited into the adjoining corridor where Calrissian and Boba Fett waited impatiently for him. "He's no good to me dead," grumbled the bounty hunter, clearly concerned that Jabba the Hutt would only pay a pittance for Solo's corpse. Vader reassured Fett that his investment was still intact, then answered Calrissian's rather bold question regarding the fate of the Princess and the Wookiee. The information that neither of them would ever be allowed to leave Cloud City seemed to surprise the baron, though Vader had much worse plans for both Rebels before his scheme was finished. It seemed Calrissian could stand a little reminder that he was no longer the ultimate authority over his insignificant municipality. **"Perhaps you think you are being treated unfairly?"** asked Vader, the simple question loaded with a thousand dire implications. The baron swallowed, then managed a weak denial. **"Good,"** Vader said. **"It would be unfortunate if I had to leave a garrison here."**

As an unplanned setting for the Skywalker snare, Cloud City possessed a serendipitous feature that greatly pleased Vader. Its industrial carbon-freezing facility was designed to encase valuable Tibanna gas for shipping, but also might be used to carbonize human beings and keep them in stasis for nearly indefinite periods of time. Since Cloud City's machinery had never been used on a living creature, Vader ordered that an elementary test be performed on Solo. If the Corellian survived, Skywalker would be subdued in the same fashion. Vader ordered an entire section of Cloud City evacuated and all doors and bulkheads sealed, except for those leading from Skywalker's likely landing point to the carbon-freezing chamber. In the interlude, the grim experiment commenced.

Solo and his companions were escorted to the chamber by a contingent of stormtroopers. Calrissian and Fett stood nearby to observe the procedure; shuffling Ugnaught workers scurried here and there among the exhaust ducts and cooling hoses. Seeing no reason for delay, Vader signaled for the captive to be placed on the hydraulic platform above the carbonite shaft. The Wookiee instantly went berserk. Several stormtroopers were pitched over the edge of the observation platform like boneless nerfs and Fett raised his blaster rifle to place a clean shot through the alien's skull. Vader slapped the weapon down. He was in charge here, and no bounty hunter could be allowed to forget that. Solo succeeded in pacifying the enraged Chewbacca, and moments later he was lowered into the dark heart of the freezing assembly. A plume of white steam and a stressed mechanical groan ensued; Vader watched with a cold, emotionless stare. As an enemy of the Empire, the Corellian pirate deserved only death, whether it was dealt out in this joyless chamber or in the decadent palace of Jabba the Hutt. Soon, a fully carbonized coffinlike slab was removed by immense durasteel tongs and pushed flat to the deck. Calrissian reported that the unorthodox procedure had worked perfectly. Vader turned to Fett. **"He's all yours, bounty hunter. Reset the chamber for Skywalker."**

Vader felt Luke as he made his way through the eerily deserted city corridors and directly to the carbonite facility. Part of that was a result of the Imperials' careful preparations, but the true orchestrator was the Force, drawing father and son together in a dance of destiny. Darth Vader stood atop a lighted platform shrouded by a haze of vapor and observed the slow, deliberate approach of his antagonistic offspring. Only a few words needed to be said. **"The Force is with you, young Skywalker. But you are not a Jedi yet."**

0100101001010010001001010000110001110100110
0011110010100011101101111011010101010100100101010101101101

01000110100100001010100101011001010010101000

The boy mounted the stairs. Vader could sense waves of arrogance and anger radiating from his foe. Eagerly, too eagerly, Luke ignited his saber. The weapon's silver pommel and humming blue blade were achingly familiar to Vader. In silent response, he switched on his own scarlet blade and the youth lunged to attack.

His son was more skilled with the energy sword than Vader had expected. A vicious, violent series of parries and thrusts forced the Dark Lord to use tactics he seldom had a chance to employ against his primitive stable of robotic training drones. **"You have learned much, young one,"** he admitted. But now was not the time for games. Darth Vader made a lightning jab and hook, sending the boy's weapon flying and forcing him down the metal staircase. Vader continued advancing, pressing Luke backwards toward the black pit of the carbon-freezing core. Too late, the youth realized his peril and tumbled down the shaft with a small cry of surprise. **"All too easy,"** muttered Vader, as he activated the freezing controls with a tug on the Force. **"Perhaps you are not as strong as the Emperor thought."**

Hot steam boiled up from the hole, but a slight movement high above caught the Dark Lord's eye. The boy tenuously hung from the cooling hoses. His prodigious jump would have been impossible without the dexterous manipulation of the Force. **"Impressive,"** Vader remarked, slashing at the tubing with his lightsaber. **"Most impressive."** Luke performed an acrobatic flip, dropped solidly to the deck, and thrust a smoke-spewing hose into his enemy's face. Vader roared in anger. In a flash, Luke had retrieved his weapon and brought it around in a sweeping cut that Vader barely deflected. **"You have controlled your fear,"** said Vader, hoping the praise would put his son off balance. **"Now release your anger. Only your hatred can destroy me."** The boy drove forward with powerful, furious blows. Vader retreated, faltered a moment at the edge of the platform, then dropped into the long shadows below.

10110100100001010100101010010100101010

1001010010100101001000100101000011000111010011101000
0011000111010011101000011010010000101010010101010010100

Vader sensed Luke searching for him through the lighted access tunnels and ultimately emerging in the reactor control room. The fact that his son seemed to know where to hunt made Vader somewhat proud of the boy's budding abilities. Whatever he might have learned in the tutelage of Obi-Wan Kenobi, however, was meaningless when compared with the limitless energies available to a dark side adept. Sith powers could move a massive generator as effortlessly as a tuft of down. Focusing his mind, Darth Vader lifted the loose bits of equipment in the room and cast them, piece by piece, at the young Jedi. Luke was nearly exhausted and his efforts to knock the machinery aside proved useless. As Vader lowered his saber, a section of metallic piping tore loose from its anchoring bolts and smashed through the wall-high transparisteel observation port overlooking the reactor shaft. With a roar, the control room's pressurized air escaped through the breach and the boy was sucked out into the abyss.

A maintenance catwalk prevented his fall. Luke pulled himself up and moved back to locate his attacker, showing admirable persistence for one whose stamina was nearly spent. Vader rejoined the fight, driving the boy back toward the end of the gantry and forcing him down to the metal deck. Vader stood triumphant, his sword tip pointed directly at Luke's throat. **"You are beaten,"** he said. **"It is useless to resist. Don't let yourself be destroyed as Obi-Wan did."** Vader was surprised when Luke batted the saber aside with his own blade, rolled, and jumped back to his feet. He was even more amazed when the boy took advantage of his overextended answering swing and landed a painful burning blow on his right shoulder. Vader bellowed in pain and, with new strength, executed three furious strikes. One stroke slashed cleanly through the gantry's instrument antennae; the second swatted Luke's saber blade aside. The final cut took his son's sword hand off at the wrist.

The fight was over. His son was defenseless, exhausted, gravely injured, and had nowhere to run. As Luke pulled himself onto the instrument cluster at the extreme end of the gantry, Vader tried to reach him with

00011101101111011101010101010101001001010101101101001000010101001010100101001010101001010010100101001000100101000100111001011001001010010100100100101000011000111010011101000001111001010001

words instead of weapons. **"There is no escape,"** he began. **"You have only begun to discover your power. Join me and I will complete your training. With our combined strength, we can end this destructive conflict and bring order to the galaxy!"**

Luke continued to resist, but Vader had been intentionally holding back one crucial piece of information for just this moment. **"Obi-Wan never told you what happened to your father,"** he offered. The injured youth swallowed the bait. "He told me enough," he spat. "He told me you killed him." Darth Vader paused for an instant. **"No. *I* am your father."**

The truth was a bracing shock that nearly overwhelmed the boy, but Vader persisted. **"Search your feelings. You *know* it to be true."** Luke cried out in blind denial, a sound of hollow, abandoned agony. **"Luke,"** Darth Vader continued, using his son's given name for the first time in their fight. **"You can destroy the Emperor. He has foreseen this. It is your destiny. Join me, and together we can rule the galaxy as father and son!"**

This standoff was pointless, and Luke would have to realize that. **"Come with me,"** he tried again. **"It is the only way."** With those words, however, something seemed to change in Luke's vanquished demeanor. The boy looked up, locked eyes with his father, and stepped off the edge of the platform into yawning nothingness. Vader quickly moved forward to watch him fall, and caught sight of the body as it disappeared into a side exhaust vent. Abruptly, the Dark Lord turned and headed back along the gantry in the direction of the shuttle landing pad.

He sensed through the Force that his son had not perished. Reports from his officers of Calrissian's treachery and the *Millennium Falcon*'s escape were distressing, but far from devastating. One of the first things that had been done to the smuggling ship upon its arrival at Cloud City had been a subtle sabotage of its hyperdrive motivator. The *Falcon* would rescue Luke and the *Executor* would retrieve the *Falcon*, a sat-

isfying end to a needlessly frustrating day. Vader's personal shuttle touched down in the *Executor's* landing bay and the Dark Lord headed immediately for the bridge.

Admiral Piett greeted him and delivered an update on the chase. "They'll be in range of our tractor beam in moments, my lord." Darth Vader trusted in his men to draw tight this simple snare. **"Good,"** he replied. **"Prepare the boarding party and set your weapons for stun."** Vader moved toward the panoramic observation windows at the front of the bridge and looked out at the tiny darting dot that represented the fleeing freighter. He could sense that Luke was aboard.

Reaching out, Vader established a mind-to-mind link with his progeny. *Luke . . .* he thought. He was pleased when the response came. *Father.* The boy had already accepted reality. It was not too late to bring him around. *Son. Come with me.* Luke seemed to have intentionally broken off the link, but Vader sent out another appeal. *Luke. It is your destiny.*

From behind him, Vader heard Piett's command to make ready for the tractor beam. The bridge came alive with muted whistles as data screens and positioning sensors came online. One instant the *Millennium Falcon* was in the targeting crosshairs; a moment later it had shot forward and disappeared into hyperspace. Darth Vader observed the startling event with thoughtful contemplation, then turned and strode from the bridge. Admiral Piett watched him raptly, his face ashen with the absolute terror of a condemned man on his way to the executioner's gallows.

The admiral was lucky. Vader gave him an indefinite stay of execution while he reflected on his son's fate and weighed the balance of destiny. The encounter had left an indelible mark on the Dark Lord's buried spirit. In the middle of a lengthy meditation he received a call from his personal Noghri honor guard, which had been surreptitiously scouring Cloud City for several items of note. Darth Vader shuttled back down to Bespin and followed the sinewy aliens into a blistering smelting core. Amid steaming heaps of scrap, several repulsive Ugnaughts were busily pawing through boxes of reclaimed waste that had been flushed out of the city's lower air shafts. It was a simple matter for a Sith Lord to locate the unusual cast-off trophy and wrest it from the gaggle of squealing subhumans. Vader returned to the *Executor* clutching both objects in his black gauntlets.

Under direct orders from the Emperor, Vader's next stop was the remote planet Wayland. The forested globe looked unremarkable from orbit but Darth Vader knew that Palpatine's private storehouse and trophy room lay deep within the stone heart of Mount Tantiss. The shriveled Emperor was waiting impatiently in the mountain complex's throne room. Vader reported to his master and dutifully presented him with a box. As the malevolent wizard expectantly lifted the lid, Vader felt a brief stab of regret, since he had hoped to transfer both items to his retreat on Vjun, but the Emperor had overridden his wishes. Showing all his damaged teeth in a smile of depraved rapture, Palpatine reached inside and removed Luke Skywalker's lightsaber and severed right hand. One more prize for the vaults, or considering Mount Tantiss's operational cloning chamber, perhaps something more.

Over the next weeks a replacement for the original Death Star began to take form above the obscure forest moon of Endor. Darth Vader returned to his private castle on Coruscant so that he could promptly respond to his master's wishes and simultaneously keep one eye on the furtive scheming of his reptilian rival, Prince Xizor. Palpatine seemed to enjoy pitting Xizor and Vader against one another. The only pleasure the Dark Lord found in their frequent encounters was his idle fantasy of squeezing the Falleen prince's throat until the man's lizardlike vertebrae snapped and shattered.

Not long after Vader's arrival in Imperial City, Xizor approached him with a critical piece of intelligence: the location of a hidden Rebel shipyard amid the Bajic sector's Vergesso Asteroids. The Falleen was undoubtedly hoping to use the information to curry favor with the Emperor, but the Sith Lord refused to allow his competitor even the smallest advantage. Darth Vader erased all records indicating Xizor's news of the shipyard's whereabouts and reported the valuable information to Palpatine himself. The Emperor, pleased, ordered his servant to depart immediately for the Bajic sector and smash the insurgents' clandestine hideaway.

The *Executor* and three smaller Star Destroyers cut the Rebel shadowport to ribbons. Eager for some hands-on destruction, Darth Vader climbed into his signature TIE fighter, one of the only Imperial vessels to have survived the debacle at Yavin, and engaged the oncoming X-wings. After a long absence from the cockpit, the Dark Lord was a bit rusty behind the controls, a weakness that could have been exploited by any marginally competent Rebel pilot. There were none. Vader blasted nearly a dozen starfighters to molten fragments without once taking a serious hit to his energy shields. The only worthy adversary he had faced in years had been his son at Bespin. He knew the two of them were destined to cross paths once again.

After the lopsided victory, Vader contacted the Emperor from the *Executor*'s communication's vault. His heart seized with hot, burning fury when he saw who was standing next to Palpatine in the holographic viewframe: Prince Xizor. Palpatine blandly congratulated his servant on his success, then subtly admonished him for not bringing up Xizor's key role in the discovery of the Rebel base. The quiet Falleen's complacent smirk of triumph was far more irritating than any public rebuke.

Upon his return to Imperial Center, Vader sensed that he had lost a measure of influence with Palpatine. His master was now prepared to move ahead with a plan formed largely at Xizor's suggestion that seemed reckless, but the Emperor loved its devious nature. The idea was to trick the Rebels by allowing their Bothan agents to capture a freighter carrying vital data on the new Imperial Death Star. If all worked

as planned, the Rebels would think that they had time to attack the still incomplete battle station, the trap would be sprung, and the Rebellion would be crushed. Vader voiced his overwhelming objection in as deferential a tone as possible, but was not surprised when Palpatine ignored him and proceeded.

The Bothans succeeded in capturing the freighter and transferring its computer core to a safe-house on Kothlis. Interestingly, Vader learned through his spies that Luke Skywalker had just been abducted on Kothlis by a group of Barabel bounty hunters. He doubted the two events were uncon-nected. Vader headed for the planet with all possible speed to pay off the Barabels and collect his son, only to discover that Luke had escaped from the bounty hunters' stronghold only hours before. Something useful did come out of the journey, however. One of the surviving Barabels confessed that a second bounty had been posted on Luke's head—Xizor's bounty—which would be paid only if the human merchandise met one grisly condition: it was a corpse.

Vader was enraged. This latest plot went far beyond mere courtly sparring. Prince Xizor was trying to murder Vader's potential successor. The Dark Lord contacted the treacherous Falleen and ordered him to keep away from Skywalker or suffer the dire consequences. Vader's son, however, didn't need his father's protection. Luke and his companions infiltrated Imperial City and destroyed Xizor's luxu-rious castle with a thermal detonator, nearly killing the devious prince. The Falleen aristocrat retreated to his skyhook, a tethered satellite high above Coruscant's atmosphere, and prepared to blast the flee-ing *Millennium Falcon* into phosphorescent fragments.

For Vader, that marked the beginning of the endgame. As his TIE squadrons unleashed dazzling devas-tation, the Sith Lord opened a channel to the skyhook. He reminded Xizor that he'd been warned not to interfere with Skywalker and gave the doomed prince exactly two minutes to surrender himself into

Imperial custody. Disdainful to the last, Xizor refused to respond. When the last second ticked away, Vader gave his turbolaser gunners permission to fire. The dying skyhook looked eerily beautiful as it unfolded into a blossom of fire.

The *Falcon*, with Luke Skywalker aboard, escaped to the safety of hyperspace. The temporary loss was but a minor one in Vader's eyes.

Time passed, and the second Death Star floated gracefully in space above a verdant emerald globe. Fine tendrils of plasteel curled across the half-completed superstructure like tiny pointed teeth biting into flesh. Lord Vader's shuttle, escorted by an honor guard of TIE fighters, approached the hangar bay and settled down on the polished deck with a thud. The Dark Lord disembarked and Moff Jerjerrod, the bureaucrat in charge of the battle station's construction, rushed forward to greet him with fawning words.

"You may dispense with the pleasantries, Commander," Vader snapped. **"I am here to put you back on schedule."** An expression of horror crossed Jerjerrod's face and he began to spout a string of weak excuses and empty assurances. Darth Vader was unimpressed and quickly came to the point: Palpatine. "The Emperor's coming here?" gasped the Moff. **"That is correct, Commander,"** replied the Sith Lord. **"And he is most displeased with your apparent lack of progress."** Vader would not have thought it possible for the man to look any more terrified, but Jerjerrod somehow managed. He promised a marked improvement in the progress of construction and Vader left him with a chilling reminder of the price of failure. **"The Emperor,"** he snarled, **"is not as forgiving as I am."**

Unlike with Vader's surprise arrival, Jerjerrod had plenty of advance warning for Palpatine's visit and was well prepared. Hundreds of officers, soldiers, and stormtroopers stood at rigid attention in the hangar bay and thousands of Imperial vessels patrolled the space around the Death Star in tight show for-

mations. Vader and Jerjerrod knelt on the deck, eyes downcast, as Palpatine tottered down the shuttle ramp. "Rise, my friend," the Emperor said to Vader, ignoring Jerjerrod entirely. As the two Jedi walked the length of the bay, Vader informed his master that the battle station would indeed be finished on the original timetable. The Emperor expressed pleasure and once again brought up the Skywalker matter. "In time, he will seek you out," he assured his servant. "And when he does, you must bring him before me." Palpatine paused, savoring his absolute mastery over everything within his sight. "Everything is proceeding as I have foreseen it." His evil laughter echoed hollowly through the cavernous chamber.

The Emperor set himself up in the Death Star's throne room, spending most of his time in private conference with his advisors and viziers. Vader was keeping abreast of the latest reports filtering in from the military and from Imperial Intelligence, most of which claimed to have pinpointed a massive armada of Rebel warships assembling near Sullust. Palpatine's call finally came, and Vader dutifully reported to his master's chambers. "Send the fleet to the far side of Endor," the Emperor commanded. "There it will stay until called for." Vader objected as respectfully as he could, pointing out the questionable wisdom of leaving the battle station open for a quick strike when the Rebels were gearing up for some unknown offensive. Palpatine overruled him. His master was clearly holding back critical information and only provided the cryptic comment, "Soon the Rebellion will be crushed and young Skywalker will be one of us." The Emperor ordered his obedient servant to shuttle back to the orbiting *Executor*.

Aboard the flagship, Vader continued to monitor Rebel fleet movements and oversee the daily comings and goings of the Death Star's supply shuttles and equipment barges. The activity was mundane and monotonous until the arrival of yet another nondescript *Lambda*-class standard Imperial shuttle. The Dark Lord sensed the vessel's approach before he saw it; one life-essence aboard it stood out like a bolt of

electricity against a backdrop of mud. Could his son have returned so soon? Vader hurried over to the clearance station, where Admiral Piett stood watching the small craft's approach on a monitor screen over a technician's shoulder. Vader interrupted without preamble. **"Where is that shuttle going?"** Piett provided the *Tydirium's* destination and clearance code, pointing out that everything seemed quite normal. Sensing his lord's concern, Piett offered to keep the ship in a holding pattern. **"No,"** Vader commanded. **"Leave them to me. I will deal with them myself."**

Vader considered the matter and decided he had better report the information to Palpatine. It would be unseemly to appear to hold back information. Vader returned to the battle station and entered the throne room, empty now save for Palpatine and his red-robed bodyguards. The Emperor looked up with annoyance. "I told you to wait on the command ship," he said peevishly. Not intimidated, Vader went ahead with his report. Palpatine showed no surprise that a Rebel shuttle had landed on the forest moon but seemed taken aback by the news that Luke Skywalker was one of the passengers. **"I have felt him, my master,"** offered Vader. "Strange that I have not," responded Palpatine. "I wonder if your feelings on this matter are clear, Lord Vader." Vader took a breath and responded in the affirmative. "Then you must go to the Sanctuary Moon and wait for him," ordered his master. "His compassion for you will be his undoing. He will come to you, and then you will bring him before me."

Less than a day elapsed before Vader received a call from the commander of Endor's surface garrison. His shuttle touched down on the landing platform as an Imperial AT-AT pulled up to one of the three docking collars ringing the structure's closest support column. Vader met the Imperial officer in the egress corridor on the lower deck. Behind the man, flanked by stormtroopers, stood Skywalker. The haughty commander turned his captive over to his lord's custody and handed over the boy's lightsaber with a disdainful flourish. Darth Vader ordered him out of their presence, leaving father and son alone in the sterile stillness of the empty passageway. Vader broke the silence.

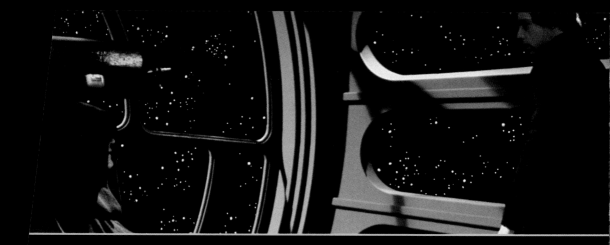

"The Emperor has been expecting you," he remarked. "I know, Father," conceded the boy, placing special emphasis on the final word. Vader seized on the small acknowledgment. **"So. You have accepted the truth."** Luke, however, took the conversation in a direction he hadn't anticipated. "I've accepted the truth that you were once Anakin Skywalker, my father," he said and went on to expound upon the core of goodness he claimed was still locked inside Darth Vader's armored shell. Luke's words were uncomfortably biting and ignited a tiny spark inside that Vader thought he had extinguished long ago.

As Vader pondered what had been said he ignited the lightsaber he held within his black gloves, examining its buzzing green blade. **"Obi-Wan once thought as you do,"** he mused. **"You don't know the power of the dark side. I *must* obey my master."** Luke made one more appeal to the Anakin Skywalker of yore and was met with a final rebuke. **"It is too late for me, Son. The Emperor will show you the true nature of the Force. He is your master now."** Stormtroopers filed in to take the prisoner to the shuttle, their white boots clattering on the floor plates. Luke looked up with a mixture of regret and pity. "Then my father is truly dead," he declared quietly.

Vader brought Luke directly to the Death Star's throne room. The turbolift doors whirred open to reveal a grim chamber of dissonant light and deep shadows. Atop the highest platform, Palpatine waited in his grand command chair. He watched their approach with satisfied pleasure. "Welcome, young Skywalker," he gloated. "I have been expecting you." With a trivial twitch of his fingers Luke's wrist shackles unlatched and clanked to the floor. A moment later the motionless royal guardsmen standing near the turbolift vacated the room at their master's command. Only the three Jedi remained. Luke was free to move—or to attack—at any time.

"You won't convert me as you did my father," Luke declared. The Emperor rose from his throne and slunk closer. "Oh no, my young Jedi," he countered. "You will find it is you who are mistaken . . . about a great many things." He spat out the final words with palpable hatred. Luke remained outwardly calm. "You're wrong," he stated serenely. "Soon I'll be dead, and you with me." The Emperor seemed to glow with evil glee. He triumphantly revealed his foreknowledge of the impending Rebel attack. Luke was clearly shaken but continued his verbal sparring. Darth Vader was finally stirred to speak. **"It is pointless to resist, my son,"** he said. Palpatine reveled in his arrogant gloating, and Vader suddenly realized what a virtuoso his master was at emotional manipulation. After the Emperor had eliminated all hope, Luke would have no recourse but to attack in furious desperation. And then the dark side would seize the boy in its unbreakable grip.

Within a short time the Rebel armada dropped from hyperspace in the vicinity of the battle station. X-wings, B-wings, Mon Calamari cruisers, Corellian corvettes—Vader had never seen such a large concentration of enemy vessels committed to a single engagement. Fortunately, the Death Star's impenetrable defensive shield was undiminished. As the Rebels scattered to avoid the invisible barrier, Admiral Piett and the other fleet commanders emerged from Endor's shadow and launched multiple wings of TIE fighters. Palpatine took his potential apprentice to the observation window for a ringside seat overlooking the fiery carnage.

Luke watched the bright flashes as his friends and comrades died in the cold vacuum above the forest moon. Palpatine, once again seated in his chair, gently patted Luke's captured lightsaber with his right hand. "You want this, don't you?" he said to the boy. "Strike me down with it. Give in to your anger!" The repeated goading was beginning to take its toll on Luke. Vader watched intently as the Emperor played his trump card. Keying the throne's intercom, Palpatine ordered the superlaser gunners to fire on the Rebel vessels. A lance of green destruction speared forth from the Death Star's focusing dish and a lumpy Mon Cal cruiser disintegrated with a silent flare.

"The Alliance will die," hissed the Emperor. "As will your friends." Vader sensed his son wouldn't be able to hold his anger in check much longer. "Take your weapon!" urged Palpatine. "Strike me down with all of your hatred, and your journey toward the dark side will be complete!" Luke looked at him, jaw clenched, then reluctantly turned back toward the window. But the final bout of needling had proved to be too much. The Skywalker anger at last came to the fore and Luke whirled about, using the Force to call his saber to his waiting hand. Igniting the blade, he swung it down with all his strength toward Palpatine's head. Darth Vader reacted with lightning speed and intercepted the stroke with his own weapon. As the sabers sparked and sizzled, Palpatine cackled with crazed merriment.

Luke attacked like a raging zealot, cutting and slashing with abandon. His frenzied charge threw Vader off balance and sent him staggering down the lighted staircase. The Emperor chuckled and praised the abrupt turn in fortunes, but Luke used the brief interlude to regain control of his seething emotions. He switched off his lightsaber. "I will not fight you, Father," he said as Vader slowly mounted the stairs. The Dark Lord drew near, close enough to strike, but Luke refused to respond. **"You are unwise to lower your defenses!"** roared Vader suddenly, bringing his saber up in a gutting slice. Luke powered up his weapon and blocked the blow, making a few more defensive parries before executing an athletic reverse somersault up to an overhead catwalk well beyond Vader's reach.

Again the young Jedi Knight allowed his anger to bleed away. "Your thoughts betray you, Father," he said. "I feel the good in you. The conflict." Vader felt anger rise in him at Luke's damaging intimations in front of Palpatine and even more at the thought that Luke might possibly be right. **"There is no conflict,"** he replied coolly. **"If you will not fight, then you will meet your destiny!"** On the final word, he threw his lit saber in a cartwheeling spin toward the catwalk's ceiling supports. The energy blade sheared cleanly through the reinforced metal and the elevated structure collapsed to the deck.

01001100011101001110100000111100101000111011011110110101010101
10110100100001010100101010010100101010100101001010100101001000100101010000

The Emperor clapped his hands with delight. Vader prowled through the wreckage to find Luke, who appeared to have gone to ground in the thick darkness between the squat columns of machinery. Vader could sense his son's presence and sense his turbulent feelings. **"Give yourself to the dark side,"** he called out. **"It is the only way you can save your friends."** A swell of feeling from Luke indicated he was on the right track. **"Yes,"** he went on. **"Your thoughts betray you. Your feelings for them are strong. Especially for. . . ."** Vader paused, not quite believing his initial reading but arriving at an inescapable and astonishing deduction. ***"Sister*. So, you have a twin sister. Obi-Wan was wise to hide her from me."** Luke remained silent. **"If you will not turn to the dark side,"** Vader speculated, **"then perhaps she will."**

His son's anguished, inarticulate scream—and flood of pure hot rage—took Vader by surprise. He thrust his saber up in just enough time to avoid a death blow. Wild-eyed, Luke drove forward furiously and recklessly, his undisciplined swings throwing off sparks where they glanced off the railing around the uncovered core shaft. The Dark Lord could do nothing but back away. Luke's unchecked hatred forced Vader onto the turbolift bridge and down to his knees. With a labored grunt of exertion and a roar of green fire, Luke severed his father's mechanical wrist. Chest heaving, the boy stood trembling, his weapon pointed at his progenitor's prone form. Vader was centimeters from death.

"Good, good!" cackled the Emperor as he approached the pair. "Your hate has made you powerful. Now fulfill your destiny and take your father's place at my side!" The seductive words triggered a fundamental change in Luke. He looked at the wires sprouting from the smoking stump of Vader's arm, then slowly clenched his own artificial hand. Drawing himself up, he switched off his weapon and turned to face his enemy. "Never," he said, throwing his saber handle aside. "I'll never turn to the dark side. You've failed, Your Highness. I am a Jedi, like my father before me." The Emperor's mouth turned down in a dissatisfied scowl. "So be it . . . Jedi."

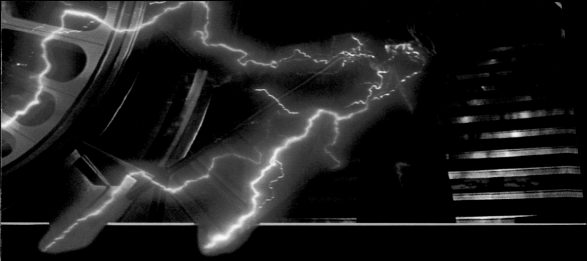

Palpatine raised both hands threateningly and the air seemed to crackle with suspended energy. "If you will not be turned," he warned, "you will be *destroyed.*" Creepers of electric current poured from his fingertips and ripped into the boy with shocking violence. Luke staggered backwards, grabbed a metallic container for support, and finally dropped to the ground in unimaginable pain. Voltage coursed through his skeleton and a thousand blue sparks pierced his flesh. Writhing in excruciating torment, Luke looked up pleadingly at Vader, who had struggled to his feet and was now standing by his master's side. "Father, please," he begged. "Help me." Though Vader appeared stoically callous, his inner thoughts surged in confusion.

The Emperor shut off the pyrotechnics and for a moment it appeared as if he might spare his victim, but his yellow eyes grew even harder. "Now, young Skywalker," he proclaimed, "you will die." Concentrated lightning even more intense than the last barrage flooded Luke's prostrate body and the boy screamed in the throes of his agony. Darth Vader looked from his son to his master and back again. At last he arrived at a life-changing determination. The Lord of the Sith picked up Palpatine with his injured limbs and hefted him high over his head. As malignant energy crawled across the skin of his life-supporting armor, he hurled the sinister despot down the bottomless core shaft. The Emperor's life force rushed out in a ravaged blur and Vader fell to the floor, weakened, wheezing, and dying.

Luke dragged his father to a shuttle hangar. Imperial officers, gunners, and stormtroopers rushed about in a state of edgy agitation over the Rebel attack and seemed to pay the pair little mind. Luke finally faltered under the weight and eased the body onto a metal spacecraft ramp. He knew Vader wouldn't last much longer. **"Luke,"** gasped the sickly voice within the nightmare helmet, **help me take this mask off. Just for once, let me look on you with my own eyes."** Carefully, with some trepidation, the young Jedi released the mechanism's rear holding clamps. With a hiss of equalized pressure, the false face lifted away.

100101000011000111010011101000001111100101

110100000111101010101011011010010000101010010101001100011101001110100000

1001110100000111100101000011101101111011010

ANAKIN SKYWALKER: THE STORY OF DARTH VADER

The air felt cold on Anakin Skywalker's face and his damaged eyes could barely focus in the harsh light. The dying man blinked weakly and took a shallow, unassisted breath. His son stared back with concern—and love—in his face. **"Now . . . go, my son,"** Anakin groaned, forcing the words through his rapidly stiffening lungs. **"Leave me."** Luke was unwilling to be orphaned so soon after regaining his father. "No," he begged. "You're coming with me. I've got to save you." Anakin attempted to smile through the hideous scar tissue of his ravaged face. **"You already have, Luke,"** he reassured his son. **"You were right about me. Tell your sister . . . you were *right.*"** The assertion escaped his parted lips in a final, rattling whisper. His eyes closed softly and Anakin Skywalker, the last of the old Jedi warriors, merged his spirit with the harmonious light of the Force.

The remaining vestiges of the tyrant known as Darth Vader were immolated in a funeral pyre in the Endor moon forest. As in a scene from ancient legend, Luke lit the primitive wooden bier with a flaming torch and watched solemnly as it blazed. Pure fire illuminated the darkness even as it consumed the mask, cape, and armor that had once belonged to the Dark Lord of the Sith. Glowing sparks and flakes of ash wafted up to the celebrating stars. Darth Vader was no more. After years of confinement, Anakin Skywalker was finally free. And as Luke gazed off to one side, he could make out the shimmering spirits of Ben Kenobi, Yoda, and his father, together again in the Force.

Just Toys made this dimensional Vader carrying case,
similar to one that Kenner had made years earlier, to
hold 20 of its Star Wars bendable figures.

III: TWENTY YEARS OF
DARTH VADER COLLECTIBLES

No one would ever accuse Darth Vader of being cuddly or cute. He certainly wasn't heroic in the accepted sense through most of his existence. He wasn't close to being colorful: his look was nearly 100 percent monochromatic, as was his booming voice. Despite all that, just about anything with a Darth Vader image has been highly collectible since the first *Star Wars* merchandise dribbled out in 1977.

The image of Darth Vader—whether on an inch-high plastic figure inside a Japanese candy box, a full-size dressed mannequin that lights up and costs $5,000, or a Dutch billboard used to promote *Star Wars* trilogy videos—is about as recognizable worldwide as that of Santa Claus, and the jolly old elf had quite a head start.

Vader's image is everywhere: model kits, stickers, push-button games, cutout masks, stamps, paint-by-number kits, origami, spring-wound toys, medallions, kites—and so much more, as shown by this chapter's list of two decades of Vader collectibles from apparel to watches. The appeal of Darth Vader items is fairly simple to understand. Vader is the arch-villain and easily the most forceful and recognizable character in the *Star Wars* saga. So it's little wonder that, from the start, merchandisers have wanted to make Vader watches, bedspreads—even baby booties. Why do fans buy Darth Vader action figures? So they can take them home and constantly trigger pleasurable memories of the films. That, at least, might be a psychologist's explanation. But there's another: because they're cool!

Some of the earliest items with Vader's image came from Factors Inc., which was one of Lucasfilm's first licensees. It hit the jackpot with *Star Wars*. The earliest Vader items included a metal pin-back

It was a marriage that had to happen: Star Wars *and Pez. But even Jedi would have to think twice before opening their mouths to willingly let Darth Vader fire pellets into them—even if they are sugary candy.*

The earliest badges, T-shirts, and related licensed items from Factors Inc. managed to misspell the last name of the Dark Lord. The design was never produced in a corrected version, and no one knows what happened to the miscreant who slipped in an "a" instead of an "e."

badge, a mirror on a chain, cloth patches, a T-shirt, and even a canvas tote, all with a blue star field–filled circle, an illustration of Vader's helmet and mask and the phrase "Darth Vadar Lives." Yes, Vad*ar*. They were in such a rush to get everything out that they misspelled the Dark Lord's last name and no one caught it in time. There isn't any indication that the Factors folks were subjected to a Vader-like choke hold. The products never had a second run with a corrected spelling and they remain oddities, but they aren't worth any more—or less—than if the name had been spelled correctly (about $5 to $25).

Even though Darth wasn't included in Kenner's first shipment of action figures (the Early Bird assortment had four heroes), the Vader action figure has been a mainstay of the under-four-inch line since the first twelve figures were issued on cards. In fact Vader is one of the only figures that—without change—appeared on every different card variation that Kenner produced between 1978 and 1985, from *Star Wars* to Power of the Force. One of the last figures to be produced in that line was that of Anakin Skywalker as he appears in spirit form at the end of *Return of the Jedi*. The most valuable figure is the earliest Vader that, like the earliest Luke Skywalker and Ben Kenobi figures, has a double-telescoping lightsaber with a needle-fine tip that extends from the figure's arm. It's possible that the double-telescoping Vader exists only as salesmen's samples, since the design was simplified to a single-telescoping saber early in production. Mint on a perfect card backing, such a figure would command more than $1,500—perhaps a lot more.

Several Vader variations have appeared in the latest incarnation of the Power of the Force line, from the regular bulked-up figure to a Vader FX with built-in light-up lightsaber. In 1998, Kenner/Hasbro released a long-sought but difficult to produce small Vader action figure with a removable helmet that shows a scarred Anakin Skywalker. The company has also remade its classic twelve-inch Darth Vader action figure, in regular and electronic versions, and a special fourteen-inch version with removable

001

helmet and electronics. Accompanying this book is the first-ever large collector figure of Anakin Skywalker as he appears at the end of *Jedi*.

Kenner reintroduced its old-style Vader in the Toys "Я" Us exclusive Classic Edition four-pack in 1995. It also made two differently posed Vaders in its short-lived metal Action Masters series, harking back to the various tiny Vader metal figurines in the also short-lived Micro Collection of 1982.

In Japan, under sublicense from Kenner in 1978, Takara's Darth Vader action figure was one of three (C-3PO and the stormtrooper were the others) that were slightly resculpted. Takara also produced a set of four eight-inch plastic action figures on a bubble card, including a fairly detailed Vader. In recent years, these rare figures have skyrocketed in price and would be hard to find for less than $400. In sealed, mint condition, they could cost hundreds more.

Related to the action-figure line were vehicles such as Darth Vader's TIE fighter, both original (a rare department store version came with a thin cardboard "battle scene" backdrop) and Collectors Series. There was also a die-cast metal version of Vader's TIE fighter. The original issue had wings that were too small and not many were made; mint on the card, that version has sold for $1,500 and up. The regular version is worth about $45 to $60. Kenner produced a Vader-head action figure carrying case (later reproduced by Just Toys for its Bend-Ems figures), with several department store variations containing figures. The case was also used in a packaging test for vacuum-metalized C-3PO cases, and some of the gold Vader cases have made it to the collectors market, where they command $150 and up.

Another unusual piece was the Darth Vader utility belt, made by Kenner Canada, along with Luke Skywalker and Princess Leia belts. These ugly plastic belts with suction-cup guns were never author-

The original large-size Kenner action figure (boys don't play with "dolls") was sublicensed by Denys Fisher for the United Kingdom market.

1010010100101001010010001001010000110001111
0001110110111101101010101010101001001010101011

ized by Lucasfilm, and when Kenner U.S. asked to sell them too, Lucasfilm said to stop selling them altogether. Ugly yes, but rare too, so one in a decent box commands several hundred dollars. Also in the strange but true category was Kenner's Darth Vader SSP van and a similar van model kit from MPC. At least they were made of black plastic and had a sort of menacing look.

One early favorite item is a colorful Kenner Darth Vader bop bag from 1978. Made of vinyl and accompanied by a patch kit, this Vader couldn't be defeated unless you squeezed the air out of him, because he bounced back every time you connected with a punch. Or you could pull down part of the Sith Lord's mask with the Darth Vader Switcheroo, which was a wall switch plate that incorporated a light switch as part of the mask.

There were lots of coloring books and some attractive paint-by-number kits of Vader (one even glowed in the dark). But the Emperor's evil henchman always dressed in basic black with very few colorful accessories, so there wasn't a whole lot to color. One of the nicest arts and crafts items was CraftMaster's 1978 3-D Darth Vader Poster Art. In addition to red, yellow, and light blue marking pens, the set contained a 17-inch by 22-inch poster, a tube of glue and a "die-cut parts sheet" that could be used to assemble a three-dimensional Vader helmet and mask. There are detailed, illustrated twenty-step assembly instructions on the back, including "coloring hints" that suggest a green Death Star. "You can't make a mistake since the finished poster is an expression of your unique personality," the package copy helpfully explains. (Price today is about $25 to $35.)

Also in the crafts area, Lee Ward made two different Vader "suncatchers," metal frames in which colored plastic was melted in the oven to produce a stained glass effect. There were also latch-hook rug and pillow kits that Lee Ward produced, in Vader head and full-body designs. More recently, Craft House created a plastic silver-metalized Vader medallion, which could be given an antique look with the included wash.

1010010101010

Costumes and masks have always been popular items among fans. These range from the original boxed Ben Cooper vinyl and plastic kids outfits ($25 to $35) to the recent Rubies costumes in child to adult sizes. (Ben Cooper also made a Vader playsuit and "fun poncho.") Don Post Studios/Party Professionals was there at the start with a plastic kid-size mask of Vader. Today the line includes a full-size glass-fiber, museum-quality mask made from an original used in the filming of *The Empire Strikes Back*. It retails for around $1,200; a heavy plastic version sells for about a tenth of that price. Masks have been made in paper, cardboard, vinyl, and rubber.

At the top of the price range is a full-size Vader mannequin from Rubies, complete with cape, mask, and hard glass-fiber parts—and it lights up, too. It sells for around $5,000. Illusive Originals has produced an eerily realistic, full-size Vader bust. It includes Anakin's head the way it looked when Luke removed his father's breathing mask. The helmet and top part of the mask hang on a separate pedestal. In 1997, Riddell came out with an amazingly detailed 45 percent scale version of the three-part Darth Vader "reveal" mask and helmet.

And on it goes, from electronic toys that will let you sound like Darth Vader, to kits that let you build models of him (one actually "breathes"), to banks and billfolds where Darth will protect your money, to posters and all kinds of clothing including Vader Underoos, to jewelry, party goods, linens, and towels—in short, just about everything except Darth Vader Really Dark sunglasses (Lucasfilm turned that one down twenty years ago).

The worldwide fascination with things Vaderish is strong, and if you have any doubts, just browse through this list of twenty years of Vaderana.

APPAREL

UNITED STATES

Jacket with "Darth Vadar lives" [sic] patch
Bright Red Group, 1977

Windbreaker with "Darth Vadar lives" [sic] patch
Bright Red Group, 1977

Darth Vader SW socks
Charleston Hosiery, 1977

Darth Vader glitter T-shirt
Factors, 1977

Darth Vader T-shirt
Factors, 1977

"Darth Vadar Lives" [sic] T-shirt
Factors, 1977

Vader helmet and X-wing T-shirt
Factors, 1977

Black leather belt with enameled Vader buckle
The Leather Shop, 1977

Darth Vader brass buckle
The Leather Shop, 1977

SW black or brown leather belt
with enameled Vader buckle
Lee Co., 1977

Vader nightgown
Wilker Bros., 1977

Darth Vader ESB socks
Charleston Hosiery, 1980

Darth Vader suspenders
Lee Co., 1980

ESB black or brown leather belt
with enameled Vader buckle
Lee Co., 1980

Darth Vader thermal Underoos
Union Underwear, 1980

Darth Vader Underoos
Union Underwear, 1980

Vader pajamas (short sleeves)
Wilker Bros., 1980

Vader pajamas (white with blue sleeves and pants)
Wilker Bros., 1980

Vader robe
Wilker Bros., 1980

Darth Vader ROTJ socks
Charleston Hosiery, 1983

ROTJ fabric belt with Vader buckle
Lee Co., 1983

Vader gloves
Sales Corp. of America, 1983

Vader mittens
Sales Corp. of America, 1983

Vader scarf
Sales Corp. of America, 1983

Vader sweatsuit (gray with black sleeves and gray pants)
Sales Corp. of America, 1983

Vader sweatshirt (sleeveless gray hooded)
Sales Corp. of America, 1983

Vader sweatsuit (white and red with red pants)
Sales Corp. of America, 1983

Vader Warm-up suit (long sleeve top and long pants)
Sales Corp. of America, 1983

Darth Vader SW Galaxy I (art by Joe Smith) sweatshirt
American Marketing, 1994

Darth Vader SW Galaxy I (art by Joe Smith) T-shirt
American Marketing, 1994

Lord Darth Vader necktie
Ralph Marlin, 1994

Vader black and white stipple T-shirt
Changes, 1995

Vader video art T-shirt
Changes, 1995

Darth Vader THX video cap
Fresh Caps, 1995

Darth Vader video cap
"Never underestimate the power . . . "
Fresh Caps, 1995

Vader embroidered shirt
Ralph Marlin, 1995

Vader silk necktie
Ralph Marlin, 1995

Vader silk necktie in tin box
Ralph Marlin, 1995

Vader's Retreat necktie
Ralph Marlin, 1995

SW video art necktie
Ralph Marlin, 1995

Darth Vader embroidered denim jacket
SW Insider, 1995

Darth Vader "Imperial Wear" T-shirt
Changes, 1996

"Darth Vader Lives" patch T-shirt
Changes, 1996

Vader and Vader's TIE vintage ringer T-shirt
Changes, 1996

*Left: Having a bad hair day? Nobody would notice—
or if they did, would never dare to poke fun—when you're
wearing this saucy logo cap from Fresh Caps.*

*Right: Vader is never afraid to say what he thinks,
so this T-shirt both recruits for the Imperial Forces and
gives more than a hint of what lies ahead. No subliminal
advertising here.*

Vader head with blue and orange highlights T-shirt
Changes, 1996

Vader "I want you" T-shirt
Changes, 1996

Vader vintage ringer T-shirt
Changes, 1996

"Darth Vader Lives" cap
Fresh Caps, 1996

Darth Vader cap
Fresh Caps, 1997

Darth Vader character cap
Fresh Caps, 1997

Darth Vader injection mold mesh cap
Fresh Caps, 1997

Darth Vader injection mold brushed cotton cap
Fresh Caps, 1997

Darth Vader Force T-shirt
Freeze, 1997

Darth Vader repeat pattern silk boxers
Ralph Marlin, 1997

Darth Vader denim shirt "The Dark Side"
Nieman Marcus, 1997

Lord Vader T-shirt
Winterland, 1997

Vader pajamas with Al Williamson art
Wormser, 1997

Vader pajamas with long pants
Wormser, 1997

Vader pajamas with shorts
Wormser, 1997

FRANCE

Vader sweatshirt, yellow
MSD International, 1980

MEXICO

Vader sweatshirt
Amate Textile, 1983

ESB black or brown vinyl belt with enameled
Vader buckle
Tudor, 1980

SWEDEN

Vader with red circle on white T-shirt
Wright and Co., 1983

BANKS/WALLETS

UNITED STATES

Vader ceramic bank
Roman Ceramics, 1977

Vader combination bank
Metal Box Ltd., 1980

Vader silver-plated figure bank
Towle, 1981

Vader figure bank
Adam Joseph, 1983

Vader nylon coin holder
Adam Joseph, 1983

Vader nylon pocket pal
Adam Joseph, 1983

Vader nylon purse
Adam Joseph, 1983

Vader vinyl billfold
Adam Joseph, 1983

Vader vinyl wallet
Adam Joseph, 1983

Vader bust savings bank
Thinkway Toys, 1994

Vader electronic talking bank (catalog packaging)
Thinkway Toys, 1996

Vader electronic talking bank (try me box)
Thinkway Toys, 1996

AUSTRALIA

Vader plastic head bank
Commonwealth Savings Bank of Sydney, 1983

CANADA

Vader bust savings bank
Thinkway Toys Canada, 1994

Vader talking bank
Thinkway Toys Canada, 1996

ENGLAND

Vader change purse
Touchline Productions, 1983

Darth Vader ceramic money box with chocolate coins
Kinnerton Confectionery, 1997

Above: An early version of the Dark Lord dominates this color saturated necktie from Ralph Marlin. The original illustration, by concept artist Ralph McQuarrie, graced the cover of the first paperback printing of the Star Wars *novelization.*

BED AND BATH

United States

SW Lord Vader bedspread
Bibb Co., 1977

SW Lord Vader bedsheets
Bibb Co., 1977

SW Lord Vader blanket
Bibb Co., 1977

SW Lord Vader curtains
Bibb Co., 1977

SW Vader beach towel
Bibb Co., 1977

SW Vader hand towel
Bibb Co., 1977

SW Vader washcloth
Bibb Co., 1977

Darth Vader/Boba Fett reversible pillowcase
Bibb Co., 1980

ESB Darth's Den bedspread
Bibb Co., 1980

ESB Darth's Den bedsheets
Bibb Co., 1980

ESB Darth's Den blanket
Bibb Co., 1980

ESB Darth's Den curtains
Bibb Co., 1980

ESB Lord Vader bedspread
Bibb Co., 1980

ESB Lord Vader bedsheets
Bibb Co., 1980

ESB Lord Vader blanket
Bibb Co., 1980

ESB Lord Vader curtains
Bibb Co., 1980

ESB Lord Vader's Chamber bedspread
Bibb Co., 1980

ESB Lord Vader's Chamber bedsheets
Bibb Co., 1980

ESB Lord Vader's Chamber blanket
Bibb Co., 1980

ESB Lord Vader's Chamber curtains
Bibb Co., 1980

ESB Lord Vader's Chamber sleeping bag
Bibb Co., 1980

ESB Vader beach towel
Bibb Co., 1980

Darth Vader figure pillow
Adam Joseph, 1983

Darth Vader/C-3PO reversible pillowcase
WestPoint Stevens, 1997

Darth Vader bath towel
WestPoint Stevens, 1997

Darth Vader beach towel
Franco, 1997

Darth Vader sleeping bag
Nieman Marcus, 1997

BOOKS AND RELATED

United States

Darth Vader's activity book
Random House, 1977

ESB storybook (hardcover)
Random House, 1980

ESB storybook (softcover)
Scholastic, 1980

Darth Vader bookmark
Random House, 1983

Vader bookplates (box of 50)
Random House, 1983

The Glove of Darth Vader
Bantam, 1992

SW: From Concept to Screen to Collectible (hardcover)
Chronicle Books, 1992

SW: From Concept to Screen to Collectible (softcover)
Chronicle Books, 1992

Vader die-cut bookmark
honeycomb-like hologram pattern
Fantasma, 1992

Vader tassel bookmark
Antioch, 1995

SW: A New Hope hardcover novel
with video art cover
Ballantine, 1995

"Shadows" cardboard Vader bookmark
Bantam, 1996

SW: The Toys postcard book
Chronicle Books, 1996

SW Flip Book
Funworks, 1996

SW Mighty Chronicle book
Chronicle Books, 1997

Darth Vader's Mission: The Search for the Secret Plans
Funworks, 1997

Left: Who would even think of trying to pry open this double combination tin bank protected by the image of Lord Vader? Metal Box Ltd. produced it in 1980.

Right: If only one Star Wars *character is desired by a licensee to sum up the trilogy and make a visual statement, it is almost always Vader, as shown on a cover for a recent Scholastic storybook.*

ITALY

ESB storybook (hardcover)
Random House, 1980

JAPAN

ESB storybook (hardcover)
Random House, 1980

BUTTONS

UNITED STATES

3" Vader SW button "Darth Vader"
Factors, 1977

3" Vader SW button (poster image)
Factors, 1977

3" "Darth Vadar Lives" [*sic*] button
Factors, 1977

Darth Vader 1.5" button
SW Fan Club, 1978

3" Vader ESB button
Factors, 1980

2" Vader ROTJ button, sold loose or carded
Adam Joseph, 1983

Vader badge
AH Prismatic, 1994

Time Warner audio books Vader button
Time/Warner, 1994

ENGLAND

2" Vader button with flashing eyes
Starfire, 1983

GERMANY

Vader button
APS Schumacher, 1983

JAPAN

2" SW Vader button (plastic)
Factors, 1977

2" ROTJ Vader "The Saga Continues" button
Rapport Co., 1983

CERAMICS

UNITED STATES

Darth Vader ceramic tankard
California Originals, 1977

Vader ceramic picture frame
Sigma, 1983

Darth Vader ceramic figurine
Sigma, 1983

Darth Vader ceramic mug
Sigma, 1983

Vader ceramic mug (black)
Applause, 1995

Darth Vader collector's stein
CUI, 1995

Mug with pewter Vader medallion
CUI, 1996

Vader ceramic mug (metallic)
Applause, 1997

ENGLAND

Darth Vader art mug
Downpace Ltd., 1996

COSTUMES

UNITED STATES

Darth Vader fun poncho (blue or red packaging)
Ben Cooper, 1977

Darth Vader playsuit
Ben Cooper, 1977

Lord Darth Vader cape with hood and mask
Ben Cooper, 1977

SW Lord Darth Vader costume and mask
Ben Cooper, 1977

Vader plastic face mask
Ben Cooper, 1977

Vader helmet (original with sticker)
Don Post, 1977

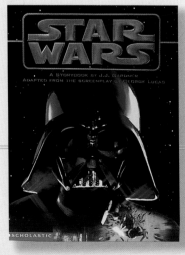

Britain's Cliro would really have had an amazing product in 1978 if the bath bubbles poured from its figural container would have resembled Vader's helmet. They didn't, of course, and the fruity aroma would have knocked Darth for a loop.

Vader helmet (later versions)
Don Post, 1978–97

ESB Lord Darth Vader costume and mask
Ben Cooper, 1980

Darth Vader costume pattern
McCall's, 1981

ROTJ Lord Darth Vader costume and mask
Ben Cooper, 1983

Darth Vader deluxe child costume
Rubies, 1994

Darth Vader value priced
Rubies, 1994

Darth Vader adult costume
Rubies, 1995

Darth Vader jumpsuit with PVC mask
Rubies, 1995

Darth Vader PVC mask (child)
Rubies, 1995

Darth Vader rubber mask
Rubies, 1995

Darth Vader teen zone costume
Rubies, 1995

Deluxe Darth Vader fiberglass helmet
Don Post, 1996

Darth Vader costume kit
Rubies, 1996

Darth Vader classic action helmet
Don Post, 1997

Darth Vader PVC mask (adult)
Rubies, 1997

Darth Vader miniature helmet
Riddell, 1997

ENGLAND

Darth Vader costume set
Acamas Toys, 1983

Darth Vader playsuit
Dejjertoys, 1995

MEXICO

Vader costume
Promotora Textil, 1997

JAPAN

Darth Vader rubber mask
Ogawa, 1983

COMPUTER RELATED

UNITED STATES

Vader mouse pad
MouseTrak, 1994

ENGLAND

Vader on gantry mouse pad
The Mousepad Co., 1997

Vader vs. Obi-Wan mouse pad
The Mousepad Co., 1997

Vader with outstretched hand mouse pad
The Mousepad Co., 1997

SINGAPORE

Vader mouse pad
Pepsi, 1997

CRAFTS

UNITED STATES

"Darth Vadar Lives" [sic] iron-on
Factors, 1977

Darth Vader and TIE fighter glitter iron-on
Factors, 1977

Vader, full figure iron-on
Factors, 1977

Darth Vader 3D poster art
CraftMaster, 1978

Darth Vader Lives poster art
CraftMaster, 1978

Darth Vader glow-in-the-dark paint-by-number set
CraftMaster, 1980

Darth Vader and TIE fighter iron-on
Factors, 1980

Vader head in circle iron-on
Factors, 1980

Darth Vader latchhook pillow kit
Lee Wards, 1980

Darth Vader latchhook rug kit
Lee Wards, 1980

Darth Vader (full body) suncatcher
Lee Wards, 1980

Darth Vader (head) suncatcher
Lee Wards, 1980

Vader rubber stamp
Adam Joseph, 1983

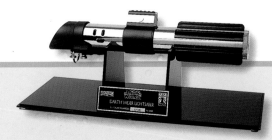

*Left: A weapon for a more civilized time? There is
nothing very civil about the way that Vader wields his
lightsaber, shown here in an exact replica from the
craftspeople at ICONS.*

*Right: Vader seems really frosted (or at least the glass
does), one of the Imperial Forces set of glasses from
Crystal Craft in Australia.*

Darth Vader suncatcher
Fundimensions, 1983

Darth Vader medan craft set
Craft House, 1996

Darth Vader medallion promo from Toy Fair
Craft House, 1996

Vader figural rubber stamp
Rose Art, 1997

CUPS/GLASSES

United States

Darth Vader tumbler #4 (of 8)
Coke, 1977

Darth Vader tumbler #4 (of 8) (smaller than above)
Coke, 1977

Darth Vader tumbler #4 (of 8)
Coke/7-11, 1977

Darth Vader tumbler #4 (of 8)
Coke/Majik Market, 1977

Darth tumbler limited collectors edition
Coke, 1979

SW/Darth Vader glass
Coke/Burger King, 1980

ESB/Darth Vader glass
Coke/Burger King, 1980

ESB/Darth Vader glass test series (indented base)
Coke/Burger King, 1980

Vader child's plastic mug
Applause, 1997

Plastic drink cup with Vader poseable figural topper
KFC (Hawaii), 1997

Plastic drink cup with Vader poseable figural topper
FAO Schwarz (Las Vegas), 1997

Vader 7-11 stores Big Gulp cup
Pepsi, 1997

Darth Vader large drink cup
Taco Bell, 1997

Australia

Darth Vader plastic tumbler
Pizza Hut, 1995

Darth Vader frosted character glass
Crystal Craft, 1996

Canada

Plastic drink cup with Vader poseable figural topper
Taco Bell, 1997

Darth Vader large drink cup
Taco Bell, 1997

England

Vader drink cup
Pepsi, 1997

Mexico

Darth Vader cup with lid and flex straw
Pepsi, 1997

Darth Vader sports bottle with blue lid and flex straw
Pepsi, 1997

Vader Pepsi glass
Pepsi, 1997

Slender Vader Pepsi glass
Pepsi, 1997

FILM, VIDEO, AND SLIDES

United States

SW THX Trilogy boxed set (Vader image, pan and scan)
Fox Video, 1995

SW THX VHS video (Vader image on cover, pan and scan)
Fox Video, 1995

SW Trilogy widescreen boxed set (Vader image on cover)
Fox Video, 1995

SW THX laserdisc (Vader image on cover)
Fox Video, 1995

Darth Vader edition 70 mm film original
Willits, 1995

SW Trilogy Special Edition VHS boxed set
(Vader cover, pan and scan)
Fox Video, 1997

SW Trilogy Special Edition VHS
(Vader cover, widescreen)
Fox Video, 1997

SW Trilogy Special Edition laserdisc set (Vader cover)
Fox Video, 1997

Canada

SW Trilogy widescreen boxed set (Vader cover, slipcase)
Fox Video, 1995

Above: A silverized Darth Vader mug from Applause makes a fine container for a hot cup of java, or some of Aunt Beru's cool blue milk.

Left: Vader in pewter tops this collector's stein from CUI, complementing an original piece of art from illustrator Jason Palmer. Vader was one of three characters immortalized (Ben Kenobi and Chewbacca were the others) in the first ever ceramic Star Wars tankards from California Originals in 1977.

FOOD RELATED

UNITED STATES

Darth Vader card game from Burger Chef fun meal
Coke/Burger Chef, 1977

Lord Darth Vader card #15 (from GM cereal)
General Mills, 1977

Vader sticker (from GM cereal)
General Mills, 1977

Darth Vader card #5 (of 16)
Wonder Bread, 1977

Vader ESB trading card
Burger King/Coke, 1980

Vader photo card, Whatchamacalit candy bar 6-pack
Hershey, 1980

ESB Vader candy head
Topps, 1980

ROTJ Vader candy head
Topps, 1983

C-3PO cereal box with Darth Vader mask on back
Kellogg's, 1984

Darth Vader card #8 (of 10) from C-3PO's cereal
Kellogg's, 1984

Vader/Anakin spinner toy
KFC (Hawaii), 1997

Darth Vader 1-liter Pepsi bottle label
Pepsi, 1997

Darth Vader 2-liter Pepsi bottle label
Pepsi, 1997

Darth Vader 2-liter Caffeine Free Pepsi bottle label
Pepsi, 1997

Darth Vader 2-liter Pepsi bottle label—half width
Pepsi, 1997

Darth Vader 2-liter Caffeine Free Pepsi label—half width
Pepsi, 1997

Darth Vader 3-liter Pepsi bottle label
Pepsi, 1997

Darth Vader 20 ounce Pepsi bottle label
Pepsi, 1997

Darth Vader 20 ounce Caffeine Free Pepsi bottle label
Pepsi, 1997

Darth Vader Pepsi soda can
Pepsi, 1997

Darth Vader Pepsi 12-pack box
Pepsi, 1997

Darth Vader Pepsi 24-pack box
Pepsi, 1997

Darth Vader bagged PEZ
PEZ, 1997

Darth Vader carded PEZ
PEZ, 1997

Darth Vader pizza take-out box
Pizza Hut, 1997

Darth Vader paper food bag
Taco Bell, 1997

AUSTRALIA

ESB jelly candies in Vader header card
Red Tulip, 1980

Wrapper for ROTJ Iced Treat with Jedi Jelly
Pauls, 1983

Vader miniature and ROTJ backdrop from kids meal
Pizza Hut, 1995

Darth Vader carded PEZ
PEZ, 1997

CANADA

Vader circular card from York peanut butter
Metric Media, Inc., 1980

Vader Pepsi 12-pack box
Pepsi, 1997

Darth Vader carded PEZ
PEZ, 1997

ENGLAND

Darth Vader SW popsicle wrapper
Lyons Maid, 1977

Vader punch out mask from ice cream packages
Lyons Maid, 1977

Darth Vader ESB popsicle wrapper
Lyons Maid, 1980

Lord Darth Vader black cherry yogurt cup
Dairy Time, 1983

Darth Vader chocolate egg
Kinnerton Confectionery, 1997

Vader shaped box of jelly candies
Kinnerton Confectionery, 1997

Vader tin of jelly candies
Kinnerton Confectionery, 1997

Darth Vader 2-liter Pepsi bottle
Pepsi, 1997

Darth Vader 2-liter bottle 2-pack box
Pepsi, 1997

Darth Vader Pepsi can
Pepsi, 1997

Darth Vader candy head
Topps, 1997

Doritos 6-pack bag
Walkers, 1997

Assorted Doritos snack bags
Walkers, 1997

GREECE

Darth Vader bagged PEZ
PEZ, 1997

HOLLAND

Darth Vader carded PEZ
PEZ, 1997

ITALY

Darth Vader Pepsi can
Pepsi, 1997

MALAYSIA

Darth Vader popsicle wrapper
Walls, 1980

MEXICO

Cremigos chocolate cookie wrapper
Gamesa, 1997

Darth Vader figurine from assorted cookie boxes
Gamesa, 1997

Emperador (chocolate) cookie box
Gamesa, 1997

Emperador chocolate cookie wrapper
Gamesa, 1997

Frutana strawberry cookie wrapper
Gamesa, 1997

Grageitas cookie box
Gamesa, 1997

Sabrosas large cookie box
Gamesa, 1997

Half liter bottle with Vader label and Vader cap
Pepsi, 1997

1-liter bottle with Vader label
Pepsi, 1997

2-liter bottle with Vader cap
Pepsi, 1997

Caramello Poffets snack bag
Sabritos, 1997

Doritos snack bag
Sabritos, 1997

Pink Vader bubble gum
Sonrics, 1997

Purple Vader shaped bubble gum
Sonrics, 1997

NEW ZEALAND

Darth Vader circle sticker from Twinkies
General Foods, 1980

Vader cutout paper mask
Tip Top, 1980

SPAIN

Darth Vader figurine from Tombola chocolate egg
Chupa Chups, 1997

Darth Vader Pen Pop
Chupa Chups, 1997

Darth Vader Port-a-Chup lollipop
Chupa Chups, 1997

Darth Vader puzzle from Tombola chocolate egg
Chupa Chups, 1997

Darth Vader TIE fighter from Tombola chocolate egg
Chupa Chups, 1997

Darth Vader ice cream stick
Frigo, 1997

Alien bits snack bag
Matutano, 1997

Darth Vader Pepsi can
Pepsi, 1997

Left: Back in 1978, a British company made edible black marshmallow candies in the shape of Darth Vader's head. A little more tasty is this white and dark chocolate lollipop. It was an F.A.O. Schwarz exclusive for Christmas 1997.

Right: Darth Vader's image was captured on several of the set of 50 Coca-Cola Japanese bottlecaps as part of a 1978 promotion. The rarest caps don't have any photos; they could be redeemed for up to 100 Yen, and most were.

FOOTWEAR

UNITED STATES

Darth Vader Lives shoes
Clarks, 1977

Darth Vader shoes
Clarks, 1977

Darth Vader sneakers
Clarks, 1977

Darth Vader boots
Stride Rite, 1983

Darth Vader shoe laces
Stride Rite, 1983

Darth Vader sneakers
Stride Rite, 1983

Vader red and white slipper socks
Stride Rite, 1983

Vader white and black slippers
Stride Rite, 1983

Darth Vader sneakers
Pagoda, 1997

ENGLAND

Darth Vader slippers
British shoe, 1983

HONG KONG

Darth Vader booties
Unknown, 1980

GAMES

UNITED STATES

Vader puzzle in tray
CraftMaster, 1983

Vader gaming miniature
West End Games, 1988

Vader on Death Star gaming miniature
West End Games, 1988

Darth Vader 3D sculpted yo-yo
Spectra Star, 1994

Darth Vader card (from SW:
Customizable Card Game premiere set)
Decipher, 1995

Vader card (from introductory SW:
Customizable Card Game 2 player set)
Decipher, 1995

Vader's custom TIE card (from SW:
Customizable Card Game premiere set)
Decipher, 1995

Vader's eye card (from SW:
Customizable Card Game premiere set)
Decipher, 1995

Vader's lightsaber card (from SW:
Customizable Card Game premiere set)
Decipher, 1995

Vader's obsession card (introductory SW:
Customizable Card Game 2 player set)
Decipher, 1995

Intimidator game (with Vader's voice)
Micro Games of America, 1996

SW 2-in-1 game with Vader medallion
Micro Games of America, 1996

SW interactive board game
with Darth Vader video cassette
Parker Brothers, 1996

Darth Vader 3D sculpture puzzle
Milton Bradley, 1997

AUSTRALIA

Vader puzzle in tray
Creative Crafts, 1983

ENGLAND

Vader 150-piece puzzle
Waddingtons, 1983

JAPAN

Vader block puzzle in plastic tray
Takara, 1978

Vader 60-piece puzzle
Takara, 1978

Vader 500-piece puzzle
Takara, 1978

Of all the incongruous items that used the image of the Dark Lord of the Sith, these fuzzy baby booties from Hong Kong have to top the list.

HOUSEHOLD AND KITCHEN RELATED

UNITED STATES

Vader flying disk
Pine-Sol, 1977

Vader SW Dixie Cup box
American Can Co., 1980

Darth Vader Switcheroo
Kenner, 1980

Puffs tissue box with color-in Vader on back
Procter & Gamble, 1980

Darth Vader cake candle
Wilton, 1980

Darth Vader cake decorating kit
Wilton, 1980

Darth Vader cake pan
Wilton, 1980

Vader ESB Dixie Cup box
American Can Co., 1981

Vader SW Saga Dixie Cup box
Dixie Northern, 1982

Vader SW Saga Dixie Cup box (win a party with Vader)
Dixie Northern, 1982

Vader speaker phone
ATC, 1983

Vader head night light plug-in
Adam Joseph, 1983

Darth Vader plastic cake topper
Wilton, 1983

Vader magnet
AH Prismatic, 1994

Vader doorknob hanger
Antioch, 1996

Vader video art phone card
GTI, 1996

Darth Vader electronic holiday ornament
Hallmark, 1997

Vader metallic holiday ornament
Nieman Marcus, 1997

JEWELRY

UNITED STATES

3" "Darth Vadar lives" [*sic*] button necklace
Factors, 1977

Darth Vader scatter pin
Weingeroff, 1977

Darth Vader ring
Weingeroff, 1977

Vader barrette
Weingeroff, 1977

Vader bracelet
Weingeroff, 1977

Vader clip-on earrings
Weingeroff, 1977

Vader key ring
Weingeroff, 1977

Vader necklace (small pendant)
Weingeroff, 1977

Vader necklace (large pendant)
Weingeroff, 1977

Vader pierced earrings
Weingeroff, 1977

Vader stick pin
Weingeroff, 1977

Darth Vader ring
Wallace Berrie, 1980

Vader dangle pin
Wallace Berrie, 1980

Vader enameled pendant
Wallace Berrie, 1980

Vader brass key ring
Adam Joseph, 1983

Vader figure necklace
Adam Joseph, 1983

Vader in Flames style key chain
Creation Conventions, 1987

Vader in Flames style necklace
Creation Conventions, 1987

Vader enameled pin
Howard Eldon, 1987

Vader figure pin
Hollywood Pins, 1993

Vader hologram key chain
Third Dimension Arts, 1993

Vader key ring
AH Prismatic, 1994

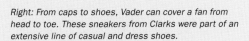

Right: From caps to shoes, Vader can cover a fan from head to toe. These sneakers from Clarks were part of an extensive line of casual and dress shoes.

Below: British Shoe produced these Vader slippers/sandals for children for the 1983 release of Return of the Jedi.

Vader small head key chain
Hollywood Pins, 1995

Vader medium head key chain
Hollywood Pins, 1995

Vader large head key chain
Hollywood Pins, 1995

Vader small head pin
Hollywood Pins, 1995

Vader large head pin
Hollywood Pins, 1995

Vader "Never underestimate . . ." pin
Hollywood Pins, 1995

Vader die-cast gold key chain (in box)
Placo toys, 1996

Vader die-cast key chain (on blister card)
Placo toys, 1996

Vader medallion key ring
Rawcliffe, 1996

Vader electronic key chain
Tiger Electronics, 1997

JAPAN

Darth Vader ring
J.A.P., 1997

LUGGAGE AND CARRYALLS

UNITED STATES

Darth Vader belt-bag
Pyramid, 1996

Darth Vader breathing belt-bag
Pyramid, 1996

Darth Vader interactive backpack
Pyramid, 1996

Darth Vader vinyl backpack
Pyramid, 1996

Darth Vader leathery backpack
Pyramid, 1997

Darth Vader leathery belt-bag
Pyramid, 1997

Darth Vader leathery duffel bag
Pyramid, 1997

Darth Vader rolling luggage
Pyramid, 1997

MODELS

UNITED STATES

Darth Vader (bust)
MPC, 1978

Darth Vader TIE Fighter (1st larger box)
MPC, 1978

Darth Vader TIE Fighter (2nd smaller box)
MPC, 1978

Darth Vader (figure)
MPC, 1979

Darth Vader Van
MPC, 1979

Darth Vader TIE fighter
MPC/Ertl, 1989

Darth Vader (figure)
MPC/Ertl, 1992

Darth Vader 1:4-scale vinyl figure
Screamin', 1992

Darth Vader 1:6-scale vinyl figure
Screamin'/Kaiyodo, 1992

Darth Vader vinyl figure model
AMT/Ertl, 1996

TIE fighter (Vader's) Flight Display
AMT/Ertl, 1996

Darth Vader TIE fighter model rocket
Estes, 1997

Darth Vader TIE fighter with paint
MPC/Ertl, 1997

ENGLAND

Darth Vader TIE fighter
Denys Fisher, 1977

FRANCE

Chasseur T.I.E. (DV TIE fighter)
Meccano, 1978

Dark Vador (bust)
Meccano, 1978

GERMANY

Darth Vader TIE-Jäger
Kenner Germany, 1978

JAPAN

Darth Vader TIE fighter
MPC/Revell/Takara, 1978

Darth Vader (1:6-scale resin)
Kaiyodo, 1992

Left: There have been a number of figural model kits of Darth Vader, including this paintable vinyl version from AMT/Ertl. Perhaps the most unusual is an early plastic Vader bust from MPC that actually made a raspy breathing sound.

Right: The first action-figure carrying case in the revived line of Kenner/Hasbro action figures carries the same Vader logo as the one on nearly all of the action figure packages.

Darth Vader (1:6-scale vinyl) small box
Kaiyodo, 1992

Darth Vader (1:8-scale vinyl)
Argonauts, 1993

Darth Vader large figure
Reds, 1994

Darth Vader large figure
Reds, 1995

Darth Vader (1:6-scale vinyl) large flat box
Kaiyodo, 1997

OUTDOOR ACTIVITY

United States

Darth Vader kite,
Spectra Star, 1983

Darth Vader Skymaster 700 kite
Spectra Star, 1994

Darth Vader figure kite
Spectra Star, 1996

Australia

Vader kite
G. & J. Barnes, 1983

England

Darth Vader action stunt kite
Worlds Apart, 1983

Japan

Darth Vader flying disk
General Mills, 1977

PARTY ITEMS

United States

Darth Vader name badges
Drawing Board, 1977

Vader small party plates
Drawing Board, 1977

Vader ESB party blowouts
Drawing Board, 1981

ROTJ Vader balloons, bag of 10
Drawing Board, 1983

ROTJ Vader punch balloons, bag of 4
Drawing Board, 1983

Vader ROTJ party blowouts (red or black header package)
Drawing Board, 1983

Darth Vader "Happy Birthday" mylar balloon
Anagram, 1997

Darth Vader party mylar balloon
Anagram, 1997

Vader small party plates
Hallmark, 1997

Vader large party plates
Hallmark, 1997

Vader table decoration centerpiece
Hallmark, 1997

PATCHES

United States

"Darth Vadar lives" [sic] patch
Factors, 1977

SW Saga Vader patch
Dixie, 1980

ESB Vader Patch (sweepstakes prize)
Kenner, 1980

Vader in Flames patch
SW Fan Club, 1980

PEWTER

United States

Darth Vader TIE fighter pewter ship with base
Rawcliffe, 1993

Darth Vader chess piece
Danbury Mint, 1994

Darth Vader pewter figurine
Rawcliffe, 1994

Darth Vader medallion
Noble Studios/SW Insider, 1995

Right: Rawcliffe's line of Star Wars *miniature pewter figurines includes this sculpting of Vader, ready for the final lightsaber duel with his son, Luke Skywalker.*

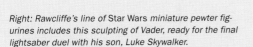

PLAQUES, SCULPTURES, AND LIMITED EDITIONS

UNITED STATES

Darth Vader Cinemacast sculpture
Kenner, 1994

Darth Vader life-size prop replica
Rubies, 1996

Darth Vader lightsaber
ICONS, 1997

Darth Vader lightsaber, James Earl Jones signature edition
ICONS, 1997

Darth Vader reveals Anakin Skywalker
limited edition sculpture
Illusive Originals, 1997

POSTERS

UNITED STATES

Darth Vader poster
Factors, 1977

Vader SW soundtrack mylar poster
20th Century Fox Records, 1977

Darth Vader door poster
Sales Corp. of America, 1983

ROTJ Vader poster
Scholastic, 1983

Vader poster for Nintendo
Nintendo/LucasArts, 1991

Vader poster for SW Galaxy cards
Topps, 1993

Litho of above
Gifted Images, 1994

Vader video art poster
Western Graphics, 1995

SHOW SOUVENIRS

UNITED STATES

Darth Vader PVC figurine
Disney, 1990

JAPAN

Darth Vader PVC figurine key chain
Kenneth Feld Pdns., 1992

Super Live Adventure Vader voice
Kenneth Feld Pdns., 1992

Vader Super Live Adventure light spinner
Kenneth Feld Pdns., 1992

Space World Exhibition memo pad
Space World, 1997

Space World Exhibition pocket memo pad
Space World, 1997

STAMPS/COINS

UNITED STATES

Vader Power of the Force coin
Kenner, 1984

SW first day cover (Vader video art)
SSCA, 1995

SW gold stamp wallet (Vader video art)
SSCA, 1995

SW gold stamp wallet (QVC version)
SSCA, 1995

SW silver stamp wallet (Vader video art)
SSCA, 1995

STANDEES

UNITED STATES

Darth Vader standee
Factors, 1977

Darth Vader standee
Advanced Graphics, 1994

Darth Vader with lightsaber standee
Advanced Graphics, 1996

STATIONERY/SCHOOL SUPPLIES

UNITED STATES

Darth Vader birthday card for 11-year-old
Drawing Board, 1977

Darth Vader die-cut birthday card
Drawing Board, 1977

Darth Vader
"Don't play games with me . . . Write!" card
Drawing Board, 1977

Left: Among the jacket patches for the crew of technicians working on the Star Wars *trilogy was the one known as "Vader in flames," which was adapted from a Ralph McQuarrie illustration.*

Right: From Down Under comes this vinyl pencil box with an unforgiving Vader from Creata Promotion of Australia.

Far Right: Ignore that command at your own peril! Which is probably why Manton Cork placed such a sticker on its angry-looking Darth Vader corkboard.

Darth Vader Halloween card
Drawing Board, 1977

Darth Vader "Happy birthday Earthling" card
Drawing Board, 1977

Darth Vader Official Duty Roster perky pad
Drawing Board, 1977

Darth Vader writing tablet
Drawing Board, 1977

Darth Vader notebook
Mead, 1977

Darth Vader asteroid puzzle birthday card
Drawing Board, 1980

Vader notebook
Stuart Hall, 1980

Vader in freeze chamber notebook
Stuart Hall, 1980

Vader puffy sticker
Topps, 1980

Darth Vader 4-pencil pack
Butterfly Originals, 1983

Darth Vader collectible eraser
Butterfly Originals, 1983

Darth Vader felt tip marker (red, blue, black, purple)
Butterfly Originals, 1983

Darth Vader head eraser
Butterfly Originals, 1983

Darth Vader head glow-in-the-dark eraser
Butterfly Originals, 1983

Darth Vader head magnet
Adam Joseph, 1983

Darth Vader pencil sharpener
Butterfly Originals, 1983

Darth Vader shuttle scissors
Butterfly Originals, 1983

Darth Vader tape dispenser
Butterfly Originals, 1983

Pencil with Darth Vader topper
Butterfly Originals, 1983

Scented marker/Darth head on clip (red, blue, black, purple)
Butterfly Originals, 1983

Box of 32 valentines with Vader on outer wrap
Drawing Board, 1983

Darth Vader and guards
"May the Force Be with You" card
Drawing Board, 1983

Darth Vader birthday card
Drawing Board, 1983

Darth Vader hologram paperweight
Third Dimension Arts, 1993

Vader mini box
AH Prismatic, 1994

Vader sticker
AH Prismatic, 1994

Vader with saber magnet
AH Prismatic, 1994

Darth Vader and troopers mini hologram desk art
AH Prismatic, 1995

Darth Vader Dark Lord of the Sith portfolio folder
Mead, 1997

Darth Vader Dark Lord of the Sith notebook
Mead, 1997

Darth Vader fat little wireless notebook
Mead, 1997

Darth Vader "Never underestimate . . ." fat notepad
Mead, 1997

Darth Vader "Never underestimate . . ." notebook
Mead, 1997

Darth Vader "Never underestimate . . ." portfolio folder
Mead, 1997

Darth Vader student day planner, blue/black
Mead, 1997

Darth Vader student day planner, gray/black
Mead, 1997

Darth Vader student day planner, Vader stitching on cover
Mead, 1997

Darth Vader zipper binder, blue/black
Mead, 1997

Darth Vader zipper binder, gray/black
Mead, 1997

Darth Vader zipper binder, Vader stitching on cover
Mead, 1997

Darth Vader FX pen
Tiger Electronics, 1997

Darth Vader lightsaber FX recording pen
Tiger Electronics, 1997

AUSTRALIA

Darth Vader head glow eraser
Crystal Craft, 1983

Darth Vader and Stormtrooper 3-ring binder
Funtastic, 1997

ENGLAND

Darth Vader 3-ring binder
Merlin, 1997

NEW ZEALAND

Darth Vader pens (orange or green)
BIC, 1993

TINWARE AND OTHER CONTAINERS

UNITED STATES

Darth Vader pencil tin
Metal Box Ltd., 1980

Darth Vader tin box
Metal Box Ltd., 1980

Darth Vader circle tin (small)
Cheinco, 1983

Darth Vader circle tin (large)
Cheinco, 1983

Vader with saber box
AH Prismatic, 1994

TOILETRIES

UNITED STATES

Darth Vader bubble bath
Omni Cosmetics, 1981

Darth Vader shampoo
Omni Cosmetics, 1981

Darth Vader soap
Omni Cosmetics, 1981

Darth Vader pop-up comb
Adam Joseph, 1983

Darth Vader toothbrush
Oral B, 1983

CANADA

Darth Vader soap
Omni Cosmetics, 1981

ENGLAND

Darth Vader bath bubbles (in figure bottle)
Cliro, 1977

Darth Vader bubble bath
Cliro, 1977

Darth Vader foam bath
Addis, 1984

Darth Vader galactic bath foam
Grosvenor, 1995

TOYS: ACTION FIGURE, DOLLS, AND RELATED

UNITED STATES

Darth Vader action figure (SW card)
Kenner, 1978

Darth Vader large-size action figure
Kenner, 1978

Darth Vader TIE fighter (action figure size)
Kenner, 1978

Darth Vader TIE fighter special edition with backdrop
Kenner, 1978

Darth Vader action figure (ESB card)
Kenner, 1980

Darth Vader action figure collectors case
Kenner, 1980

Darth Vader's Star Destroyer action playset
Kenner, 1980

Darth Vader action figure (ROTJ card)
Kenner, 1983

Darth Vader TIE fighter in collectors edition box
Kenner, 1983

Darth Vader action figure (Power of the Force card)
Kenner, 1984

Darth Vader action figure (long lightsaber)
Kenner, 1995

Darth Vader action figure (short lightsaber),
orange card
Kenner, 1996

Darth Vader 12" doll, dark background
Kenner, 1996

Darth Vader 12" doll, light background
Kenner, 1996

Darth Vader TIE fighter
Kenner, 1996

Darth vs. Xizor action figure set
Kenner, 1996

Darth Vader action figure, green card
Kenner, 1997

Darth Vader vs. Ben Kenobi 12" Power F/X doll set
Kenner, 1997

Electronic power F/X Darth Vader action figure
Kenner, 1997

Darth Vader action figure, freeze frame card
Kenner, 1998

Darth Vader 14" electronic doll
Kenner, 1998

Above: Kenner/Hasbro's Power FX electronic Darth Vader action figure has a light-up red lightsaber and is ready to do battle with the Power FX Luke Skywalker. The bases of the two figures join together, and both can advance, retreat, and spin around thanks to handy lever action.

ENGLAND

Darth Vader action figure (SW card)
Palitoy, 1978

Darth Vader action figure (ESB card)
Palitoy, 1980

Darth Vader action figure (ROTJ card)
Palitoy, 1983

Darth Vader action figure (tri-lingual card)
Palitoy, 1984

Darth Vader action figure (long lightsaber)
Kenner, 1995

Darth Vader action figure (short lightsaber)
Kenner, 1996

CANADA

Darth Vader action figure (SW card)
Kenner Canada, 1978

Darth Vader action figure (ESB card)
Kenner Canada, 1980

Darth Vader action figure (ROTJ card)
Kenner Canada, 1983

Darth Vader action figure (long lightsaber)
Kenner Canada, 1995

Darth Vader action figure (short lightsaber)
Kenner Canada, 1996

JAPAN

8" Vader figure
Takara, 1978

Darth Vader action figure (SW card)
Takara, 1978

Darth Vader figure (SW card, white figure background)
Takara, 1978

Die-cast Vader figure
Takara, 1978

Darth Vader action figure in box #2
Popy, 1980

Darth Vader action figure (long lightsaber)
Hasbro Japan, 1995

Darth Vader action figure (short lightsaber)
Hasbro Japan, 1996

BRAZIL

Vader action figure
Glasslite, 1988

TOYS: ELECTRONIC

UNITED STATES

Darth Vader power talker
Micro Games of America, 1995

Darth Vader mix and match walkie-talkie
Micro Games of America, 1996

Darth Vader squawk box
Tiger Electronics, 1997

Rebel Force laser game in shape of Vader
Tiger Electronics, 1997

ENGLAND

Radio control Darth Vader
Hitari, 1997

TOYS: MICRO MACHINE RELATED

UNITED STATES

Darth Vader/Bespin transforming action set
Galoob, 1994

Action fleet Darth Vader TIE (big wings)
Galoob, 1995

Action fleet Darth Vader TIE (small wings)
Galoob, 1996

Darth Vader lightsaber/trench battle
Adventure Gear (1st)
Galoob, 1996

Darth Vader lightsaber/trench battle
Adventure Gear (2nd)
Galoob, 1996

Darth Vader TIE flight controller
Galoob, 1996

CANADA

Darth Vader/Bespin transforming action set
Galoob, 1994

Action fleet Darth Vader TIE (big wings)
Galoob, 1995

Darth Vader lightsaber/trench battle Adventure Gear
Galoob, 1996

Darth Vader TIE flight controller
Galoob, 1996

Left: From the George Lucas Super Live Adventure arena show in Japan comes this Darth Vader battery-operated voice changer. When you speak into the back, a muffled sound comes out the front grill. Labored breathing works best.

Right: Japan's Takara produced this highly detailed six-inch die cast metal and plastic Darth Vader figure as part of its extensive line in 1978, when Star Wars *finally opened in Japan—13 months after its U.S. premiere. The lightsaber glows in the dark.*

TOYS: MISCELLANEOUS

UNITED STATES

Darth Vader inflatable bop bag
Kenner, 1978

Darth Vader SSP van
Kenner, 1978

Die-cast Darth Vader TIE fighter
Kenner, 1978

Darth Vader small vinyl statuette (Suncoast Video)
Out of Character, 1993

Darth Vader large vinyl statuette (Suncoast Video)
Out of Character, 1993

Darth Vader Action Master figurine (two styles)
Kenner, 1994

Darth Vader statuette with lighted base
Applause, 1995

Darth Vader vinyl doll (Vader standing on rebel helmet)
Applause, 1995

Darth Vader vinyl doll with cloth cape
Applause, 1996

Darth Vader lightsaber (red box)
Kenner, 1996

Darth Vader vinyl doll, boxed
Applause, 1997

Darth Vader lightsaber (green box)
Kenner, 1997

Darth Vader Buddy small plush doll
Kenner, 1998

CANADA

Darth Vader utility belt
Kenner Canada, 1977

Darth Vader Bend-Em/form-fitting bubble
Just Toys, 1993

Darth Vader Bend-Em/form-fitting bubble with Topps card
Just Toys, 1993

Darth Vader Bend-Em/square bubble
Just Toys, 1993

Darth Vader Bend-Em carry case
Just Toys, 1994

Darth Vader Action Master on card
Kenner Canada, 1994

Darth Vader lightsaber (red box)
Kenner Canada, 1996

Darth Vader TIE space shooter
Milton Bradley, 1996

GERMANY

Darth Vader vinyl large figurine (same as Suncoast)
Carlsen Comics, 1994

JAPAN

"Baby Vader" small plush doll
Takara, 1992

Vader mini flashlight/lightsaber (yellow, green handle)
Makura Toys, 1977

TRADING CARDS

UNITED STATES

Vader box art #0 card
Topps, 1993

Vader hologram: SWG1 Millennium Falcon factory set
Topps, 1993

Darth Vader 23 karat gold card
Scoreboard/QVC, 1995

Vader in his TIE Fighter SW Finest promo card SWF2
Topps, 1996

Vader Shadows of the Empire promo card SOTE2
Topps, 1996

Darth Vader 24 karat gold card, SW
Authentic Images, 1997

Darth Vader 24 karat gold card, ESB
Authentic Images, 1997

Darth Vader unmasked 24 karat gold card, ROTJ
Authentic Images, 1997

Vader cover gallery card C4
Topps, 1997

WALL DECORATIONS

UNITED STATES

Darth Vader window art decal
Image Marketing, 1993

Lord Darth Vader large hologram wall art
AH Prismatic, 1994

Dark Lord of the Sith (Factors poster) Chromart
Zanart, 1994

ESB advance style A Chromart
Zanart, 1994

From Concept to Screen to Collectible cover Chromart
Zanart, 1994

Darth Vader hang up
Great Scott!, 1995

Left: This 24k gold embossed card from The Scoreboard has Vader reaching out to an unseen Luke Skywalker near the end of The Empire Strikes Back.

Right: "You cannot resist the power of the Force!" says Vader, just prior to the sound of an explosion. What a pleasant way this Talking Alarm Clock from England's Spearmark International Ltd. has of waking up little children.

Far Right: If a loud alarm from the AM/FM clock radio isn't enough to wake you on a dreary morning, then a sleepy glance at the menacing visage of Darth Vader should do the trick. The battery-operated clock radio is from Micro Games of America.

Darth Vader trilogy flag
Great Scott!, 1995

SW video art small Chromart
Zanart, 1995

SW video art large limited edition Chromart (Musicland)
Zanart, 1995

Darth Vader Al Williamson litho (limited to 500)
Zanart, 1996

Darth Vader banner
Sharper Image, 1996

WATCHES AND CLOCKS

UNITED STATES

Analog with black rubber strap; gray face "SW,"
"Darth Vader," full body with saber, oval display box
Bradley Time, 1977

Analog with black rubber strap; white face "SW,"
"Darth Vader," full body with saber, stars on bezel
Bradley Time, 1977

Analog with rubber and metal strap; gray face "SW,"
"Darth Vader," full body with saber, stars on bezel
Bradley Time, 1977

LCD digital, black rubber strap; blue SW logo on white face
"Darth Vader" with saber
Bradley Time, 1980

LCD digital, black rubber strap; lenticular face "DV," "SW"
Bradley Time, 1982

LCD digital, black rubber strap; white face "Vader," "SW"
Bradley Time, 1982

Analog with black leather strap; Vader on numberless
face with X-wing and TIE second hand; snap box
Fantasma, 1993

As above but in clear plastic ball in gift box
Fantasma, 1993

As above but numbered limited edition in velvet pouch
Fantasma, 1993

Darth Vader hologram watch with rubber strap
Third Dimension Arts, 1993

Darth Vader hologram watch
AH Prismatic, 1995

Darth Vader AM/FM clock radio
Micro Games of America, 1995

Darth Vader collector's sculpted watch, carded
Hope Ind., 1996

Vader limited gold watch in circular tin
Fossil, 1997

Vader limited gold watch in Death Star case
Fossil, 1997

Vader limited silver watch in circular tin
Fossil, 1997

Vader limited silver watch in Death Star case
Fossil, 1997

Darth Vader collector's sculpted watch with Falcon case
Hope Ind., 1997

Darth Vader collector's sculpted watch
with Death Star case
Hope Ind., 1997

AUSTRALIA

Darth Vader flip-top watch, space battle package
Playworks, 1996

Darth Vader analog watch; Vader face, stormtrooper strap
Playworks, 1997

Darth Vader flip-top watch, C-3PO package
Playworks, 1997

LCD Vader watch; Vader face, TIE fighters on strap
Playworks, 1997

CANADA

Darth Vader flip-top watch
Watchit, 1997

ENGLAND

Darth Vader talking alarm clock
Spearmark, 1997

Darth Vader analog watch; Vader face, stormtrooper strap
Watchit, 1997

LCD Vader watch; Vader face, TIE fighters strap
Watchit, 1997

JAPAN

Analog with black leather strap; Vader on face,
X-wing and TIE second hand; Superlive Adventure box
Fantasma, 1993

Darth Vader hologram watch, gold trim and leather strap
Third Dimension Arts, 1993

MEXICO

Darth Vader watch included with AA 8-pack of batteries
Duracell, 1997

BIBLIOGRAPHY

I. THE EMERGENCE OF DARTH VADER
    Bouzereau, Laurent. *Star Wars: The Annotated Screenplays*. New York: Del Rey Books, 1997.
    Chernoff, Scott. Interview with Ian McDiarmid. *Star Wars Insider*, no. 37 (April/May 1998).
    Henderson, Mary. *Star Wars: The Magic of Myth*. New York: Bantam Books, 1997.
    Hull, Pete. "James Earl Jones: Speaking for Darth." *Star Wars Insider*, no. 25 (May 1995).
    Jones, James Earl, and Penelope Niven. *Voices and Silences*. New York: Charles Scribner's Sons, 1993.
    Lippincott, Charles. Transcripts of interviews of George Lucas, Ben Burtt, Ralph McQuarrie, and John Mollo.
        San Anselmo, Calif: Lucasfilm Ltd., 1977-78.
    Paley, Jane. Script for audio tour for *Star Wars: The Magic of Myth*. Produced by Visible Interactive,
        San Francisco, 1997.
    Sansweet, Stephen J. *Star Wars: From Concept to Screen to Collectible*. San Francisco: Chronicle Books, 1992.

II. THE SAGA OF DARTH VADER
    Anderson, Kevin J. *Darksaber*. New York: Bantam Books, 1995.
    Austin, Terry, adaptor. *Splinter of the Mind's Eye* by Alan Dean Foster. Milwaukie, Oreg: Dark Horse Comics, 1995-96.
    Crispin, A.C. *Rebel Dawn*. New York: Bantam Books, 1998.
    Daley, Brian. *The Empire Strikes Back*. Dramatizations for National Public Radio, 1983.
    ____. *The Empire Strikes Back*. Collected scripts from National Public Radio dramatization. New York:
        Del Rey Books, 1995.
    ____. *Star Wars*. Dramatizations for National Public Radio, 1981.
    ____. *Star Wars*. Collected scripts from National Public Radio dramatization. New York: Del Rey Books, 1994.
    Foster, Alan Dean. *Splinter of the Mind's Eye*. New York: Del Rey Books, 1978.
    Glut, Donald F. *The Empire Strikes Back*. New York: Del Rey Books, 1980.
    Goodwin, Archie, and Al Williamson. *Classic Star Wars*, nos. 1-20. Milwaukie, Oreg: Dark Horse Comics, 1992-94.
    Kahn, James. *Return of the Jedi*. New York: Del Rey Books, 1983.
    Lucas, George. *Star Wars: A New Hope*. New York: Del Rey Books, 1977.
    Macan, Darko. *Vader's Quest*. Milwaukie, Oreg: Dark Horse Comics, 1998.
    Moesta, Rebecca. *Vader's Fortress*. New York: Berkley Publishing Group, 1997.
    Perry, Steve. *Shadows of the Empire*. New York: Bantam Books, 1996.
    Slavicsek, Bill. *Death Star Technical Companion*. Honesdale, Pa.: West End Games, 1991.
    Star Wars: A New Hope. 20th Century-Fox. 1977.
    Star Wars: The Empire Strikes Back. Lucasfilm Ltd., 1980.
    Star Wars: Return of the Jedi. Lucasfilm Ltd., 1983.
    Star Wars customizable card game. Norfolk, Va.: Decipher Inc., 1995-96.
    Star Wars Galaxy Magazine, no. 11 (May 1997).
    Trautmann, Eric. *The Last Command Sourcebook*. Honesdale, Pa.: West End Games, 1994.

III. TWENTY YEARS OF DARTH VADER COLLECTIBLES
    Sansweet, Stephen J., and T. N. Tumbusch. *Tomart's Price Guide to Worldwide Star Wars Collectibles*. 2nd ed.
        Dayton, Ohio: 1997.
    Sansweet, Stephen J., and Josh Ling. "Vader Rules Collectibles." *Star Wars Galaxy Magazine*, no. 11 (May 1997).